DIAMOND
AND
PEARLS

A NOVEL

JULIEN AYOTTE

Author Photo Credit: Glenn Ruga

Copyright © 2019 Julien Ayotte

All rights reserved.

Library of Congress Control Number: 2019919863

Published in the United States by Kindle Direct Publishing

Ayotte, Julien

Diamond And Pearls: a novel/Julien Ayotte

ISBN: 9781713293651

Also by Julien Ayotte

Flower of Heaven
Dangerous Bloodlines
A Life Before
Disappearance
Code Name Lily

What people are saying about Julien Ayotte's writing:

Flower of Heaven is a fast-paced global thriller that would make a great movie...Bill Reynolds, *Providence Journal*

A Life Before is a smart, well-paced thriller that will give readers pause to rethink their own déjà vu experiences... Recommended by *US Review of Books*

Disappearance: The author has developed a strong cast of characters to include those that are smart, deadly, and believable. A solid story without the use of excessive violence, sex, and strong language...5-star review, *Readers' Favorite*

Code Name Lily: The Comet Line's and Micheline's work helping hundreds of Allied servicemen escape is truly a spectacular WWII account. Countless more people will learn of her bravery through your character, Lily... Stephen Watson, *The National WWII Museum, New Orleans*

Code Name Lily by Julien Ayotte is one of the most unique historical fiction novels I have ever read. The story is absolutely amazing, and its greatness is magnified by the fact that it actually happened. 4 out of 4 stars...*OnlineBookClub.org*

Julien Ayotte's writing is comparable to David Baldacci and Harlan Coben on the thriller scale...Jon Land, *USA Today* best-selling author

Julien Ayotte is probably the best writer of mystery thrillers in Rhode Island...Paul Caranci, best-selling author of *Wired* and *Scoundrels*

To
Pauline

CHAPTER 1

JANUARY, 2019

The doorbell rang at 44 Tiffany Lane, Attleboro, Massachusetts as the heating oil company's serviceman stood outside. Joyce Conway glanced out the glass pane next to the door, and greeted the Superior Oil repairman as she let him in. *Right on time,* she thought.

January weather in New England can be brutal. Cold temperatures, snow, sleet, rain…take your pick. Residents in the area get them all. This winter morning, Joyce had risen at eight o'clock to a fifty-two degree bedroom, and she proceeded to blast her husband Ray.

"What is wrong with you? Can't you see the furnace isn't running? It's fifty-two in the bedroom, and the thermostat in the great room shows sixty-two degrees," she barked at Ray.

Ray, a retired school teacher, sat in the kitchen with his winter bathrobe doing the daily crossword puzzle in the local newspaper over a cup of coffee, with the morning news on the TV in the background.

"I thought it felt a little cool this morning, but I didn't notice that the furnace wasn't running. After I picked up the newspaper in the driveway, where it was really cold, coming back inside felt a lot warmer."

"You'd better get down there to check the furnace. There must be a reset button or something. Maybe we're out of oil?"

"No way, Babes, we're on automatic delivery. There's no way they would cut it this close in this kind of weather. But I'll go down and take a look."

A few minutes later, Ray was back upstairs, and headed for the telephone.

"We've got a half a tank of oil. I hit the reset button, and nothing happened. I'm calling Superior right now."

Typical of most service calls today, you get a two to four hour window of when they'll show up. Fortunately, the window that morning was between ten in the morning and noon. Since the hot water heater was electric, Joyce could still take a shower while the serviceman worked on the furnace with Ray by his side, throwing in his two cents worth of input.

There's a macho thing about guys talking with repair guys, thinking their knowledge in such matters would be bolstered by the association. Truth be told, Ray didn't know the first thing about how oil-fired furnaces functioned, except for the little red button inside the unit that begged you to push it. It just seemed like the right thing to do, and if it worked, you would proudly walk back upstairs looking like a hero.

Ray met the service guy once Joyce saw him in, and asked him nicely to thoroughly wipe his feet on the carpet facing the front entrance. The snowfall from the previous night was messy, and Joyce had just finished vacuuming and swiffering the floors the day before.

"Not a problem, sir. I brought some protective cloth shoe covers so I wouldn't mess up your floor. My name is Tom. Let's take a look at your furnace and get you some heat."

"Follow me, Tom. I'm Ray. You'll have to excuse the bathrobe at ten o'clock, but I usually shower and dress after my wife does, and this little disruption this morning set us back a bit."

"No need to worry, sir, I'm looking forward to doing the same someday."

Ray led the repairman down the stairs to the basement.

"Wow, how do you keep the cellar looking so clean?" Tom asked as his first glance of the spacious basement revealed a gray painted floor and walls with metal shelving along the perimeter of the outer walls, and absolutely nothing else on the floor except the oil furnace on one side and the electric hot water heater at the opposite end of the basement.

"Most basements I go to have an obstacle course I need to go through, just to get to the furnace."

"We try not to accumulate junk that gets put down here. If we're not using the item anymore, chances are we'll never need the item again, so we get rid of it. We keep shelves for household supplies and soda, the Christmas stuff around the corner, and a treadmill and weights near the stairs, that's about it," Ray answered.

The serviceman quickly removed the cover to the furnace, pushed the infamous red button, and the exhaust fan went on. Many modern homes conveniently eliminate constructing a chimney in favor of ductwork that shoots the furnace's air out the side of the house rather than out through a chimney on the roof. Under normal working conditions, a minute or so after the fan goes on, the fan motor triggers the furnace to go on. In this case, the fan just kept running, but the furnace failed to start.

"Hah, looks like you've got a blocked or frozen line in the fan. The furnace only goes on if the air from the fan line goes directly outside. If the line is blocked for some reason, the furnace won't go on. If it did, all that exhaust air would probably leak out this exhaust pipe here in the basement and might find its way upstairs."

Ray listened attentively to this explanation, looking as if he understood what the repairman had just said.

"Say, you wouldn't have a glass of water I could have, would you? I'm fighting a cold, and I'd like to take a cold tablet." Tom asked.

"Sure, no problem, I'll be right back," Ray answered as he headed for the stairs to the kitchen.

No sooner had Ray started to climb the stairs, Tom made a beeline for the small cellar window at the rear of the house, and unlatched the clasp that held the window closed. Within seconds, he was back near the furnace. A minute later, Ray reappeared, carrying a glass of water.

"Thanks a lot. All I need to do is blast this tube with air to unblock it. I'll bet the cold night we had last night, and some condensation in the line, caused the line to freeze up on you. We'll get you back with some heat in a jiffy."

Within minutes, sure enough, after hitting the red reset button again, the fan went on, and a minute later the furnace started. Tom grabbed his tool box, wrote up the service call, handed a copy to Ray, and was out the door on the way to his next customer.

Sitting in his truck, Tom reached for a notebook and merely wrote, "44 Tiffany Lane, Attleboro, rear window." He then called his office from his cell phone to get his next stop. The notebook had pages of addresses in it, some crossed out, but many that were not.

Two weeks later, on a Wednesday night, Joyce and Ray Conway were getting ready to go to dinner with friends, as they normally did on Wednesdays. It was five o'clock and pitch dark at this time in January. As Ray backed the car out of the garage, and he and Joyce drove down the driveway, neither of them noticed the dark sedan parked on the side of the road across the street.

As Ray's car turned the corner from Tiffany Lane to another road, the sedan parked across from their home, still with the lights off, drove up the driveway and turned the motor off. The figure in the car quietly got out and walked to the rear of the house and the cellar window. The intruder was wearing spandex bottoms with a hooded black sweatshirt and black sneakers and a dark unmarked baseball cap. She pushed the cellar window open, slid her slender body through the small opening, and landed on the basement floor below. She then quickly closed and locked the window, and with a flashlight in hand, walked briskly toward the staircase.

The intruder cleverly stayed to the rear of the house, which faced a grove of trees and no other house in sight. The one level home had only a few rooms that faced the rear of the property, and she quietly entered the master bedroom first, and closed the door behind her.

There were two pieces of furniture with drawers, a large dresser and an armoire with double doors. Assuming the larger dresser was for the woman of the house, she began rummaging through each drawer, searching for valuables. In the second drawer, she found a rather large jewelry box tucked under some undergarments at the rear of the drawer. She quickly opened the box and dumped its contents into an empty sack and moved on.

In the next drawer, under more clothing, she found an envelope with nearly $500 in cash and stuffed the envelope in her pants pocket beneath the spandex she wore, ever so careful not to disturb other items in the drawer. The small jewelry box sitting on top of the dresser didn't interest her at all. *No one puts expensive jewelry in a box sitting proudly in plain view,* she rationalized.

Next, she moved to the armoire and ran her hands under clothes in every drawer. Men aren't too creative when it comes to hiding things. She uncovered a few wrist watches and nothing more, so she left the room and quietly paced to the other side of the house into what appeared to be an office. The blinds were shut tight, and her flashlight would not carry any light outside to the front side of the house facing the street.

Bingo! The top drawer on the left revealed an envelope with another $500 in cash.

"Don't push your luck, Syd. It's time to go," she mumbled to herself.

Within ten minutes, she had been in the house and out the back door, leaving the dead bolt lock unlocked, but locking the lower single bolt as she left, all this time wearing tight-fitting rubber gloves on both hands. She backtracked to her car, turned the car around in the driveway, still with the lights off, and slowly descended the inclined driveway before she turned on the car lights and disappeared into the night.

Later that evening, Joyce and Ray returned home from dinner, and got ready to relax and watch television for a while. It was nine o'clock. Neither noticed the unlocked deadbolt on the rear door, and neither had occasion to go into Joyce's jewelry box or Ray's desk drawer that night.

The following morning was a different story.

CHAPTER 2

THE MORNING AFTER

Ray rose on Thursday at his usual six-thirty, drank a glass of water with his vitamins, and headed out the door down the driveway in his bathrobe to retrieve the morning newspaper. It was quite chilly that day, and Ray was anxious to get back inside. He checked the thermostat to make sure the furnace was running fine. The last thing he wanted was to be blasted again by Joyce two days in a row. She never got up that early, eight or eight-thirty was fine with her.

By then, Ray was already on his second cup of coffee, and had already logged on to his computer in his office. It was eight o'clock, and he reached for the checkbook in the right hand drawer of the desk to pay the cable bill he had received the day before. *Cheap bastards,* he thought, *they don't even give you a return envelope to mail your check anymore. And there's no way I'm paying online.*

He then opened the top left hand drawer of his desk to get an envelope to address the check he had just written. Something was wrong. Something got his attention, or was it the absence of something that he noticed?

"Where's my cash envelope?" he said out loud, but too far for Joyce to hear behind a closed bedroom door.

The envelope was gone. He waited restlessly for another half hour until Joyce burst into his office with her morning greetings.

"Morning, hon, anything new on the net?" she asked matter-of-factly, more interested in getting to the kitchen and starting her morning breakfast routine.

"Did you by any chance move my cash envelope from my desk drawer?"

"No, you can't find it? Are you sure you didn't put it somewhere else?" she asked.

"I haven't moved that envelope from the same spot in the eight years since we moved here. It's gone. There was $500 in the envelope the last time I added to it about a week ago."

"I don't know. I don't see anything out of place in here. How about you? We should check the bedroom. You've got more stuff there than I do here. I've already checked the safe, and everything is still in there. I brought the list with me of all the stuff in the safe, and that was okay," Ray added.

They both rushed to the bedroom. Joyce checked the drawer where she had her fun money, and her envelope was missing too…another $500 in cash.

"Oh, damn, Ray, somebody took my money. We've been

robbed, but how did they get in with our deadbolt locks?"

"The deadbolt in the front door was on before I went to get the paper earlier. What about the others?" he asked, as he walked out of the bedroom.

"The deadbolt for the back door is unlocked. Only the other lock is in the locked position," he yelled.

"After I went out to check the outside thermometer yesterday morning, I'm sure I relocked the deadbolt," Joyce shouted.

"I'm calling the police. Somebody broke in here when we were out to dinner last night. We were home before that, and then the rest of the night. Crap, we were only gone for a couple of hours."

While Ray made the call to the Attleboro Police, Joyce decided to see if she noticed anything else missing. Nothing seemed out of place, no drawers left open, nothing thrown to the floor. Whoever was responsible for the break-in was no amateur.

"Oh, no! Ray, get over here. My pearls, they're gone. All of my good jewelry, the box is empty. My family pearls. Oh, God, do you know what they're worth today, probably close to $100,000. They were my grandmother's from when they lived on Margarita Island in Venezuela in the early 60s."

"The police are sending a detective over. It seems we're the fifth house in the last month to have a break-in. They claim this has never happened before."

Both of them hurried to shower and get dressed before the detective arrived. Joyce still hadn't had breakfast yet. Ray ran another coffee through the Keurig, and Joyce managed to down an English muffin before the doorbell rang.

"Hi, I'm Detective Mullen. Have you been in your basement at all this morning?" he asked the two of them.

"No, neither of us has been down there. Why?" Ray asked.

"How about the back yard?"

"No, I only went out the front door, down the walk to the driveway to get the paper around six-thirty, that's it for being outside," Ray answered.

Detective Mullen walked to each entrance and tried to see if he could notice any signs of forced entry anywhere. He asked Joyce if she was certain the rear door deadbolt had been locked when they went to bed the night before.

"I'm not certain. I don't go out that way in the winter, so we never use that door. But I'm sure it was locked before this," she stated.

"Since all the rest of your deadbolts are locked, it looks like the intruder left this way, and had no way to lock the deadbolt from the outside without a key. Most burglars come in from the rear. You can't see much at night from the back of a house. Now the question is, how did he get in?" asked Mullen. "It's almost as if he had a key and just walked in," he added.

"My kids and my neighbor across the street are the only people with keys," Joyce chimed in. "And we don't have an alarm system. We didn't think we needed one with the deadbolts."

"So, tell me again, what's missing here?"

"$1000 in cash, $500 from an envelope in her dresser, and $500 from an envelope in the top drawer of my desk," Ray chimed in. "But my wife's special jewelry box at the back of the second drawer in her dresser, the whole contents are gone," Ray continued.

"When you say special jewelry box, do you mean expensive jewelry?" Mullen asked.

"An heirloom from my grandmother, a pearl necklace and ring…a $100,000 pearl necklace and ring," she answered.

"Are you folks covered for this? Do you have some kind of precious metal or jewelry rider on your homeowner's policy? Most insurance companies don't carry coverage for cash losses, and I think you need special coverage for expensive jewelry. You need to check your policy, and then call your agent to report this," Mullen added.

"This is the fifth burglary this month in the area, and I know of two more in Pawtucket, just across the line past Spumoni's Restaurant. Same MO, no signs of forced entry, no ransacking, nothing out of place. And three of the homes with deadbolts all had one deadbolt lock unlocked. There has to be something in common with all of them. I don't know what it is yet, but if you can think of anything unusual in the last few weeks, give me a call," Mullen scratched his head as he handed Ray one of his cards.

"Oh, by the way, you wouldn't have a photo of that pearl necklace would you? You never know how fast items like that get fenced real quick," he added.

"Yes, I do as a matter of fact. And we do have coverage for the pearls with Assurance Property and Casualty.

They needed several shots of the necklace and ring to include in their files with the rider to the homeowner's policy," Joyce proudly answered. "But it's not about the money, Detective, it's all I have from my grandmother, and it was my intention to pass it along to my daughter Susan one day."

"For that kind of money, I'm certain your insurance company will have some inspector following up on any leads before they dish out $100,000," Mullen said. "That's one heck of a necklace, ma'am. I didn't know pearls were that expensive?"

"Neither did I, until we had it appraised in New York by a pearl specialist. The necklace has forty pearls, natural pearls, not cultured ones, and all of them are thirteen millimeters in size, perfectly round, and pure white. I wouldn't have paid more than $200 for the necklace when the appraiser said they were worth about $80,000. That was two years ago, and the last appraisal in 2018 showed the value up to $100,000 resale value," Joyce stated.

"What's the difference between natural and cultivated pearls?" Mullen asked.

"That's cultured pearls, not cultivated, and the difference is primarily in what they are worth. I couldn't tell one apart from the other, but there are subtle differences that experts can point out to you. It's like the difference between a real diamond and one that is made of zirconia. I can't tell the difference, but try to sell the zirconia one to a jeweler. I probably should have kept them in a safe deposit box or a safe," she said.

"Don't go blaming yourself, ma'am. This guy knew

what he was doing if, indeed, all your deadbolts were locked. All the other burglaries together don't amount to as much as your pearls did. How about the other jewelry in the box?"

"I keep a list. I'll make a copy for you. Probably another $5,000 to $6,000 worth of bracelets, necklaces, and pins."

"Don't forget to include those in your call to your insurance company. We'll need one of you to come down to the station to fill out an official burglary claim in the next day or so."

Ray jumped in quickly.

"I'll be there this afternoon. Should I ask for you?"

"Sure, but any of the people will help you out if I'm not there for some reason. Try not to worry too much about this. With any luck, we might recover it all. The $1,000 in cash is another story."

Mullen told the Conways he would be taking a quick walk around the house perimeter to see if he noticed anything unusual. He left by the front door and quickly made his way around to the side of the house where there was a small cellar window. There was nothing unusual there, and no footprints in the remaining snow still on the ground. Next, he walked to the rear of the house where there was a second cellar window. He quickly pulled out his police phone and called the station.

"Get me a lab guy right away at 44 Tiffany Lane, Attleboro. We've got two good shoe prints in the snow, and I need to get a mold of these before they disappear."

He rang the doorbell again. Ray answered.

"Looks like the burglar got in through your rear cellar window. Did you leave it unlocked for some reason?"

"I never open those windows, Detective," Ray said.

"Well, based on the footprints leading to the window, the fact that it's not broken, and it's now locked again, someone unlocked it from the inside. Who else could open it from the inside?" Mullen asked.

CHAPTER 3

VENEZUELA, 1930-1965

Sure enough, the Conways' homeowners' insurance policy included a rider for certain items in Joyce's expensive jewelry collection. Because the standard language in a homeowner's policy covered personal belongings only up to a certain value, loss of high-end items, however, were not covered under a standard policy.

Joyce's pearl necklace had been appraised by a professional to the satisfaction of the insurance company. She had a copy of the documentation sent to Assurance in 2018, along with copies of photos with the appraisal paperwork. The coverage was for replacement cost, the cost of replacing the item at today's prices. Unfortunately, if the item stolen had a particular sentimental value, such as an heirloom, no replacement cost could replace the actual item. Joyce's natural pearl necklace was part of the family, an item handed down from her grandmother,

Consuelo Ortiz, to Joyce's mother, Veronica Best, and subsequently to her in 2015 when her mother died at age seventy-four from Alzheimer's.

Manuel Ortiz, Consuelo's husband, had been a pearl diver on Margarita Island, off the coast of Venezuela, for nearly thirty years, from 1935-1965, eventually dying from a pulmonary embolism at age forty-seven. Margarita Island today is considered a tourist attraction with tropical beaches and Caribbean-style resorts. But back in the 1940s, the Venezuelan island, near Curacao and Aruba, was predominantly known for maritime businesses, including pearl diving.

Ortiz dove for the Island Pearl Company from the time he was seventeen years old. He was not educated and the jobs on the island were limited for a person without many skills. Pearl diving was very risky work, and Manuel was able to make a decent living the more experience he gained from one year to the next. He knew the hazards involved, but never complained, so long as he could provide for Consuelo and Veronica, their daughter and only child.

The pay per day was high in comparison to menial wages he would earn from fishing or farming. But the risks were high as well, and pearl diving had many dangers. From repeated diving into deep water, a diver could develop decompression sickness, or he could drown due to an underestimation of dive time. Some divers would get burst ear drums or hypothermia from exposure to the cold. But Manuel had a unique skill...he could hold his breath for more than ten minutes underwater. This was an advantage he had over most other divers, because the longer he was picking up oysters on the ocean floor, the greater the likelihood he would retrieve one or more shells containing a pearl.

He would free-dive down into the salty water with a basket or bag to collect the oysters. He would scrape off as many as he could before he ran out of air and had to surface. To keep him from inadvertently floating back to the surface prematurely, he would tie a heavy stone to his leg to keep him on the ocean floor. Divers came back on the boat for lunch each day around noon as the boats dumped their load of oysters under watchful eyes. Within an hour, divers were back in the water until five o'clock in the afternoon. Early each following morning, the shells were opened. Finding a pearl brought everyone's wages up.

Margarita natural pearls in the 1930s, when Manuel was a diver, were worth only a few dollars for a 5.5 carat pearl. Some larger ones were known at times though to bring in $3000-$4000 for a single pearl that was much larger in size. Manuel managed to pocket a pearl or two on many occasions over the thirty year period that he dove. In 1965, ironically just two months before he died, he gave Consuelo a necklace with forty large pearls on it.

* * *

In today's market, the demand for natural pearls has given way to cultured pearls, formed by controlled particles inserted into an oyster on an oyster farm. This process is much less risky than deep sea diving, and produces good quality pearls, albeit in an orderly fashion. Cultured pearls are close to flawless, and if cared for properly, have a way of retaining lifelong value. High quality gems are extremely durable, the main reason Manuel passed the necklace to Consuelo to begin with. It was his intent that she in turn would someday pass the necklace onto their daughter Veronica, or Vero as she was called as a child.

In the same year, just before he died, Manuel had also given Consuelo a single natural pearl fastened to a ring to match her necklace. All of the pearls were 13 millimeters in size, pretty much the largest size for a natural pearl. Famous people like Elizabeth Taylor, Angelina Jolie, and the royal family in Monaco are said to own pearl necklaces exceeding a million dollars. Needless to say, Manuel's intent was to create an heirloom that could be passed down from generation to generation.

Manuel and Consuelo Ortiz were married in 1939, both at the age of twenty-one. While Manuel was busy diving for pearls each day, Consuelo served as the housekeeper for Enrique Sosa, the owner of the Island Pearl Company, at his large home in the town of Parlamar on Margarita Island. Wages for a maid were not good but, coupled with Manuel's diving salary, were enough for them to own a modest three-room house overlooking the beach in the small town of Caripito, a port city on the island, and near the boats where Manuel worked.

Veronica was born in 1941, a beautiful blond-haired child who was not only very pretty, but seemed to be a vacuum of knowledge as she grew. Determined to make sure Vero received the best schooling, where her parents had none, the Ortiz family sent Vero away to Caracas, Venezuela, when she was fourteen. Although she knew she

would miss her family terribly, and the quiet surroundings of the beachside living, Vero also realized that the
education she could receive in Caracas was far better than
the local schools on Margarita Island could offer. Vero
excelled in every class she took at the Colegio Cervantes,
and she ended up graduating in 1958 at seventeen years
old. Manuel and Consuelo, although very proud of their
daughter's accomplishment, realized the lack of opportunity she would have in securing a good job on Margarita Island. Vero had gained the recommendation of the
teachers at her school, and when asked by local recruiters
for good potential workers who might be interested in
working in the oil industry in Caracas, her name was most
often mentioned.

She accepted a position with Creole Petroleum Company and began a career with the Venezuelan subsidiary
of Standard Oil of New Jersey. It was here that she met
Lucas Best, an American civil engineer on assignment in
Venezuela with Standard Oil. They were both attending
the same conference in Caracas, and one thing led to another. After dating for nearly two years, Lucas' assignment
in Venezuela was ending, and he was to be reassigned to
the company's headquarters in New Jersey in 1961.

The thought of leaving Vero behind, when he was
about to leave the country, was something Lucas never
even considered. He was twenty-five and Vero barely twenty when he asked her to marry him before he returned to
the U.S. She did not hesitate to accept his proposal, and
they were married in a small church in the fishing village
of Playa Caribe on Margarita, with Vero's proud parents

beaming at the wedding. They had succeeded in giving their daughter a quality education, and her upcoming move to the U.S. was like a dream come true.

"She will have a beautiful life in America, Consuelo. Vero promised to visit us as often as she could. Lucas seems to be a nice man," Manuel said to her as they both shed tears watching their precious daughter dancing with her new husband.

Three days later, Lucas and Vero were booked on a TWA flight from Margarita Island to Newark, New Jersey. The night before, they had a quiet and emotional dinner on the beach, just outside the Ortiz residence. Manuel's diving comrades had offered to prepare the entire meal as a farewell dinner to Vero, whom they had watched grow up in front of them for nearly twenty years, and for whom they had grown fond of.

Following a meal packed with shrimp, lobster, scallops, and tuna, the highlight of the night from Manuel's buddies was an envelope for the newlyweds containing one hundred dollars in U.S. currency. Lucas and Vero were overwhelmed with such kindness.

As the night came to an end, and the co-workers bid farewell to Vero in a tearful goodbye, Consuelo asked Vero to walk the beach with her one more time. While they walked together, Consuelo said, "I don't know how many more times we will do this together, Vero, but I have something to show you that someday will belong to you."

She reached into the pocket of the sweater she wore on this cool night near the ocean, and pulled out the necklace. The pearls gleamed in the moonlight above, and the white pearls had a glint of rose color against the moonlight.

"A mãe, they are so beautiful. Was this a gift from o pai?" she asked.

"It took your father nearly twenty years to find each of these pearls to perfectly match the others. When I am old, they will be yours, and all I ask is that you keep them in the family by passing them on one day to your own daughter."

CHAPTER 4

PROVIDENCE, RHODE ISLAND 2019

Garrett Hunter, a forty- year- old jeweler in Providence, was busily washing the counters in his downtown store, Hunter Jewelry, on Dorrance Street. At eight-thirty every day, Monday through Saturday, this would be part of his morning routine. The store opened at nine in the morning amid relatively heavy foot traffic going to and from the various office buildings in downtown Providence. Having his store located at an intersection with Westminster Street greatly added more pedestrian traffic all day long…good for business.

This was a Monday morning, and that meant he had to have his $200 cash envelope ready for his weekly visitor from the mob for his "protection" fee. The local henchman had promised he would not have any trouble, so long as he continued his payments at his location.

Garrett, the father of two small children and a thir-ty-five year old wife, had a comfortable home in Warwick near the ocean, and willingly agreed to pay, if it meant peace of mind. In turn, Richie Volpe, the last mobster still living on Federal Hill, between Atwells Avenue and Broadway, would often pass hot jewelry to Garrett for a reasonable price, allowing Garrett to make a tidy profit from the resale of such items. Since he kept a separate inventory of these items, the sale of the hot jewelry nev-er got recorded anywhere, and he would pocket the net profit in cash. He would never let on to Volpe that the money he made from the sale of hot jewelry far exceeded the $200 weekly extortion money. Otherwise, his weekly protection payment would surely rise.

At nine o'clock sharp, Garrett unlocked the front door to the store and flipped the sign on the door to 'Open." Within ten minutes, Sydney Malone walked through the door and proceeded to the counter facing Garrett.

"Good morning. I'm in the market to sell a pearl necklace and ring that's been sitting in my drawer at home for probably twenty years. I was wondering if you give appraisals for pearls. I know it's kind of a specialty, and I'll be the first to admit I don't know the difference between a natural pearl, a cultured pearl, or a fake one. I do know these aren't fake, because of when I inherited them years ago. My mother wouldn't bother to put these in her will if they weren't expensive."

Sydney was a petite well-dressed woman with a phy-sique that clearly reflected the perfect shape she was in. Her long blonde hair, her dark eyes, her glittering smile, and the way she conducted herself, all had you paying attention to what she had to say. At thirty-two years old, she looked like a successful professional executive.

"Why would you want to sell something your mother left you in her will?" he asked.

"Good question. Well, I've never worn the necklace and ring in the twenty years since I got them when I was twelve, and I could use the cash to help furnish my new condo at the Westin Towers."

"Well, Madam, I'm not as much of an expert on pearls as a New York specialist might be, but let's take a look at what you have."

Sydney reached inside her large shoulder bag and pulled out an enclosed black felt jewelry box and a ring box and placed them on the counter. Garrett carefully opened the jewelry box and, to his amazement, stared at this magnificent necklace containing forty large pearls. He could tell by the age of the chain that the necklace had been around for quite a while.

He rubbed the pearls against the front of his teeth, not against the edge, which could scratch the pearl. This immediately brought a grimace to Sydney's face.

"What in the world are you doing?" she questioned.

"There are several ways to test a pearl or pearl strand to determine its real value. The tooth test is one of them. If your pearls feel gritty, not smooth, when you rub them lightly against a tooth, the pearl is clearly either a natural one or a cultured one. Simulated or fake pearls would feel smooth. Your strand of pearls is clearly either natural or cultured," he answered.

"So they are real, aren't they?" Sydney blurted with excitement.

"Yes, they are real, but there are nearly ten tests in all to determine how much they are worth. The tooth test is only one of these. I have to go through all the tests in order to give you a reasonable estimate of how much they're worth. This will take some time."

"What are we talking about here, minutes, hours, a day?" she asked with a cautious look on her face.

"It probably will take me about an hour or so, unless I get a lot of other customers walking in on me this morning. I'm all alone on Mondays. It's usually a slow day, but you never know in this business."

"Okay, I'll wait."

"The next test is the color test. Most people think a pure white pearl is the kind to own, but the most valuable ones are white with a rose overtone. When I hold your pearls up to the light, I can clearly see the rose overtone. That's good."

"So, what's the difference between a cultured pearl and a natural one? Are they worth about the same? I know nothing about this, and I'm beginning to get the feeling I really should know more," she asked.

"Pearls are the only precious gems that are produced by a living creature, an oyster. Most pearls on the market today are cultured, which means they are made at an oyster farm by inserting a small piece of shell or sand into an oyster. The oyster then secretes a silky coating around the irritant, layer by layer, until a pearl is formed. Now I'll look at the surface thickness, the luster, and then the shape and size of each pearl."

Garrett held the strand of pearls next to his bright light lamp and rolled the pearls. If the surface was thin, the pearls would blink at you because of the poor luster. This would be due to excessive wear. The thicker the pearls, the better the luster. Again, he smiled at Sydney and she knew what that meant.

"Now let's measure the size of the pearls and their shape. Perfectly round pearls are ideal. I'll roll these on the glass surface. If they are slightly elliptical, I'll be able to tell. Pearls out-of-round are less expensive, but very common. These look almost perfectly round."

He reached for his calipers and measured each pearl separately to determine their size. While the size of diamonds is measured in carats, pearls are measured in millimeters. The larger millimeters get the highest price. He shook his head as he was astounded to read the size of each pearl as identically thirteen millimeters, virtually the largest size for pearls.

"Madam, these are truly fine pearls, and I don't believe I can give you anywhere what they are likely worth. For that matter, I don't know of any jeweler in Rhode Island who could. You'd be far better off going to New York to the American Gem Society. They can tell you precisely what these are worth and who might buy them. There are no blemishes on any of the pearls, they all match in color, luster and roundness. Even the drill holes are perfectly centered."

"You don't by any chance know where they are from, the Caribbean, the South Seas, Japan?" he asked.

"No, she never told me anything about them. All I

know is that they were in her estate when she died, and that she wanted me to have them," Sydney replied.

"Did she travel a lot to any of the places I mentioned, before she died or even years ago?"

"I really don't recall. We weren't very close."

"Because it's such a large necklace, it will be much more difficult to sell, especially around here. I can probably go to $5,000 for both the necklace and the ring," he said as he gazed at the matching ring.

"We are talking cash here aren't we?" she asked.

"I've been at this location now for over ten years. I believe you'll find my reputation speaks for itself, and my check will be quite valid."

"Never mind. I'll try somewhere else. I don't have the luxury of waiting for the check to clear. The furniture store offered me a huge discount if I paid cash for the pieces I want for my condo, but only until tomorrow by noon," Sydney answered as she began to pick up the two items.

"This is Monday morning, Madam, and I just opened for the week. If you come back, say tomorrow morning at the same time, I can have the $5,000 in cash by then. I'd go to the bank myself today, but there would be no one to mind the store while I'm gone."

"I'll think about it. If I have no luck elsewhere today, I may be back in the morning," she answered. She replaced the two boxes in her bag, and left the store.

No sooner had the woman left the store, Garrett reached under the counter and pulled out a folder. He began flipping through the folder at photos of stolen jewelry provided by the police. There it was, a photo of the same necklace and ring. At the bottom of the photo was the name, Drew Diamond, Investigator, Assurance Property & Casualty Insurance Company, 342 Washington Highway, Lincoln, Rhode Island. Handwritten next to the investigator's name were the words "Estimated appraisal $100,000. Reward to anyone aiding in the recovery: $10,000."

* * *

Sydney was no fool. Hardly anyone would hide such a large pearl necklace and matching ring under clothing in a dresser if it was only worth $5,000. She knew the jeweler was low-balling her, but that was to be expected. Someone walking in off the street with jewelry to sell isn't about to get a huge offering from a jeweler. Jewelers are in the business of selling jewelry, not buying it. And the ads for "We'll buy your gold or jewelry at top prices" are usually a rip-off, she believed, mostly offering a small fraction of the item's value.

The object here was to ditch the hot jewelry as fast as possible, and go on. She would likely be back to Hunter Jewelry on Tuesday morning, but first she decided to visit Simonton's Jewelry at the Emerald Square Mall in Attleboro. That location had just been honored as the top retail store in Massachusetts by the Better Business Bureau. She had the time to see what they would offer her for the pearls, since her next real estate showing wasn't until three that afternoon.

Because working for a realtor meant house listings and showings at all hours of the day, and into the early evenings, her schedule was flexible, but left her plenty of time for her nighttime hobby. A few rough years in the real estate market in Rhode Island left Sydney seeking supplemental income to maintain her rich lifestyle. She was very cautious in her side business, and never personally met the various servicemen she used to 'unlock' new opportunities for her. Envelopes with cash were conveniently left in the mailboxes of her sources. At $200 per address, several servicemen had agreed to simply call a designated telephone number, leaving the message, "this is number 6. The address is 44 Tiffany Lane, Attleboro, rear window." On occasion, the designated rear window had been relocked by the owner, and she chalked that up as a loss. She currently had four servicemen on the payroll, so to speak.

Sydney also never used the same jewelry store twice in trying to fence jewelry. It was no wonder that she preferred finding cash over jewelry. In the recent months, she had stolen nearly $10,000 in cash, and several thousand dollars more in gold items that would likely be melted for the gold content than resold. But there was something about these pearls. Her curiosity increased by the minute as she entered Simonton's.

She used the same spiel as she had used at Hunter's. Simonton's, however, was nowhere near as forthcoming about the value of real pearls as Hunter was. And the requirement to consider buying any jewelry from a walk-in customer included proof of ownership of the item or items in question.

"I don't have that with me at the moment, but I have the insurance appraisal rider at home, and I can easily get it for you," she said.

"If you like, I can give you a ballpark figure of between $1,500 and $2,000 for the two items. But once you come back with the record of ownership we need, I can be more accurate on a price for you," Carol Simonton answered.

As she left the showroom at the mall, Sydney mumbled to herself, "Well, Mr. Hunter, I think we have a deal."

CHAPTER 5

THE CLUES UNFOLD

Drew Diamond had been a detective for the Worcester Police Department in Massachusetts for thirty-five years before retiring in 2017. For the last two years, he has been an insurance claim investigator for Assurance on high claim cases, primarily those cases involving burglaries or the massive destruction of property from a fire. His expertise in break-ins and arson cases made him a valuable asset at Assurance, and he had prevented false claims from being settled on many occasions in his two years on the job.

Drew was a widower with two grown children, a thirty-year old son, Drew Jr., and a twenty-five year old daughter, Alicia. Both children were single, but both had fiancées. Drew Jr. practiced real-estate law in Rhode Island for a small law firm in Providence, Smalley & Sons, while Alicia served as a medical representative for Dresden Pharmaceutical in Guilford, Connecticut.

A fairly stocky man, Drew had seen too many nights sitting in a parked car on stakeouts, eating fast-food sandwiches. Following open-heart surgery in 2016 to repair a defective heart valve, he knew his police detective days would soon be over. Luckily, he was able to reach the thirty-five year mark on the police force with no further incidences.

The insurance company environment was much less rigid, and left him to work on his own most of the time. A few cases that ended up in the insurance company's favor kept him in good standing with the general counsel at the company.

On Tuesday morning, after reviewing the new file on the burglary and subsequent claim from the owners on Tiffany Lane, and the potential loss to Assurance of $100,000, Drew visited the Conways. He had the Attleboro police report in his hand when Joyce answered the doorbell at ten in the morning.

"Drew Diamond from Assurance, Ma'am," he said as he pulled out his card. "Are you folks okay?"

"Well, I guess it's the feeling of being invaded in your own home that hurts probably more than the loss of my grandmother's pearls. Please come in, Mr. Diamond," Joyce answered as Ray suddenly appeared beside her.

"I've spoken to Detective Mullen, and he did tell me there's been a string of similar burglaries in the vicinity over the last month. It seems we have a new thief all of a sudden, but you are my first reported claim, and I must say, it's quite a claim," Diamond exclaimed.

"Is there a problem, Mr. Diamond?" Ray asked.

"No, not at the moment. But because of the size of the claim, I've been assigned to look into the case, and maybe, if we're lucky, get your pearls back. I'm betting that whoever stole them has no clue what they're worth. To my knowledge, those are probably the most expensive strands in the area, and I don't know a single jeweler around here who sells expensive pearls like yours. I've sent photos of them to every jeweler in New England by email, offering a $10,000 reward if someone has information about them. We always run the risk that some jeweler will buy them for a song, and then drive to New York to dump them for at least two to three times what my company is offering to get them back. If one of the jewelers does handle the pearls, he runs the risk of accepting stolen property. That's a felony, and subject to jail time," Diamond went on.

"I was about to call Detective Mullen, Mr. Diamond. He had asked me if we had any visitors in the last few weeks. The only person I could come up with was my oil serviceman who came one morning to restart our furnace. I can't think of anyone else who has been in the house, other than Joyce and our son in the last month," Ray mentioned to Diamond, "and the service guy definitely was in the basement, and would have had access to unlock the cellar window."

* * *

"Call me Jack," Detective Mullen said as he shook Diamond's hand a short while after Diamond had left the Conways. "I kind of figured I'd be hearing from you again. Did you find anything in the report that we gave you earlier today?"

"I just left the Conways and they told me that the only person entering their house in the last three weeks was their oil serviceman from Superior Oil. Maybe there's a connection with the other handful of burglaries you've had," Diamond mentioned.

Mullen picked up the file on his desk and started flipping pages.

"Well, what have we here? All six burglaries had an oil service guy in their homes within weeks of a burglary there. They're not all from the same oil company though. Do you want to take a ride, Drew? Superior Oil is about two miles from here. Did the Conways get the service guy's name off the service call sheet by any chance?"

"Tom. The guy's name was Tom," answered Diamond.

Ten minutes later, they entered the office of Superior Oil and were greeted by a cheery clerk named Louise. Mullen flashed his police badge, introduced himself, then introduced Diamond.

"Is the owner in, by any chance?" he asked.

Louise led them down the hall behind the office counter area, and knocked on the door of Jason Winter's office as she entered the partially open door.

"A member of the local police is here to see you with another gentleman, Jason."

"Good morning, gentlemen. I'm Jason Winter. How can I help you today?"

"Jason, we've had a number of break-ins over the last month, and all of them were burglarized within weeks following oil service calls to their homes by Superior and other oil company servicemen. We'd like to get copies of all your service calls in the last month, if that's possible. Maybe the same person serviced all of these homes, or some of them," asked Mullen.

"That's a big request, Detective. We have six servicemen, and they all cover a wide area of our customers. You're looking at probably a thousand calls in that time. Can you narrow it down a bit?" Winter asked.

"Are all your service calls on the computer? Because if they are, maybe you can print a list by serviceman, by date, and by address serviced. That way we can see if there is anything unusual on one of these guys."

"Detective, we do a pretty thorough background check on all our guys, and they've all been with us for at least two years, and up to twenty years for one of them."

"I understand, sir, and I would appreciate it if you didn't mention this to anyone for the time being. It might just be a coincidence, and we don't want to alarm anybody, nor are we pointing a finger at anyone…at least not yet."

"I can run that report for you right now, Detective. It'll only take about five minutes for me to sort the report in the categories you asked for, and another few minutes to print the report. I'll print it off my printer here, and no one will know what I'm doing," Winter said.

Jason Winter was a third generation owner at Superior, having assumed the reins after his father retired a year earlier, and now spent his winters in Florida. Jason was fifty years old, unmarried, and very computer savvy. He had modernized all of the company's oil delivery trucks to allow delivery information to be wirelessly channeled into the company's main computer instantly. All employees had tablets and/or smart phones, and Jason constantly sought ways to make Superior a cut above the competition. A true workaholic, the only socializing he did was playing tennis twice a week, and golfing during the summer months.

Within ten minutes, Jason stood beside his printer and picked up the twenty-five page special report he had just prepared.

"I hope you find what you are looking for, Detective, while at the same time, I hope none of my guys are involved in any of this."

As they returned to the police station, Mullen pulled out the five addresses in the Attleboro area and the two in Pawtucket where other burglaries had occurred recently. Of the seven locations with a burglary, only two had been serviced by someone from Superior Oil, including the Conways. The serviceman was Tom Holt, age twenty-five, single, and a Superior employee for three years.

Mullen circled the information and wrote down the names of the other two oil companies who had done work at the other five homes that had been burglarized. Two homes had a serviceman from Paragon Oil, and the remaining three homes a guy from Bourque Oil and Heating.

"Drew, want to make a few more trips? Maybe we can eliminate the oil guys as suspects, or find a pattern on all these break-ins that eliminates them," Mullen asked.

"If we get photos of all these guys, and flash them in

front of jewelers in the area, maybe one of them will be a match. Although, it's not every jeweler who'll look at the photos of the pearl necklace I emailed them," Diamond answered.

Later that day, the two of them had the information they were looking for from the other oil companies, and they met in Mullen's office at the station. Both Paragon Oil calls had been serviced by Bob Bragg and the other three by a Bourque Oil guy named Randy Tuttle. After Mullen entered their names on his computer, a search came up with nothing, which meant none of the oil servicemen had a previous criminal record.

"Ironically," Mullen said, "all of these guys might be too big anyway to enter a house through a cellar window, unless they all work for someone else who does the actual break-ins."

"What are you thinking, Jack?" asked Diamond.

"What if someone pays each of these guys to unlock a cellar window when they're in the basement of a house, and to merely let somebody know they did so for a price or a cut of the action? The actual burglar would never rely on just one guy to supply him with open windows, that's far too easy to discover. Spreading it around among the three of them would make it more difficult to trace," Mullen added.

As Diamond was about to leave the station, his cell phone rang.

"Mr. Diamond, this is Carol Simonton from Simonton Jewelers at the Emerald Square Mall, and I'm just now getting to my emails. I was away from the store last week, and I'm finally catching up. Anyway, I think I have a lead for you on those pearls you're looking for. A well-dressed blonde woman, very attractive I might add, came in here on Monday, and had a string of pearls and a matching ring just like the ones in the photo you emailed us last week."

"Tell me, Carol, that you have video cameras in your store?" Diamond asked as he motioned to Mullen to wait before he left the station.

"Of course we have video cameras, and I'm certain you can probably see good shots of the woman. She was facing our main counter, and that has a direct camera showing frontal shots of all our customers."

"Tell me, Carol, was this woman small, I mean petite and somewhat short?" Diamond asked.

"She was thin, but not too small, about my height I would say, five feet five inches or so."

"We'll be right over," he stated as he passed the news onto Mullen. "Jack, we may have a break. Some woman tried to fence the pearls at Simonton's at Emerald Square Mall, but she didn't have proof on her that the pearls were hers. She was going home to get her insurance binder. I doubt if she comes back there, it's pretty difficult to show proof of ownership when you don't have any. How about one more ride, just a few miles up Route 1?"

Carol Simonton greeted the two a short while later, and led them to the office at the rear of the store to a series of monitors. Carol retrieved the Monday tapes and Mullen started playing them.

"She came in around eleven in the morning or so. I'll skip the tape to that time period on Monday."

Most of the tape was blank during this time period until the customer in question appeared with the pearls. The tape showed the customer laying the necklace on a mat on the counter as she talked to Carol. When the camera showed a clear shot of the woman's face, Mullen asked Carol to freeze the tape.

"We'll need a copy of this tape right away, ma'am, or you can let me have this one and we'll get it back to you once our guys get all the information off of it that they need."

"You can take the original, Detective. I'll just load a blank tape to replace this one. Normally, a tape lasts nearly a week before I get a blinking light warning me to change the tape."

"Thank you. If we recover these, you'll get the reward from my company, as we promised. If she should return, maybe you can somehow call Detective Mullen without alerting her that something's wrong. I'm glad to meet an honest business owner who isn't lured by dealing in stolen merchandise."

Mullen handed her his card, and the two headed back to the station for the third time. The photo analysis would be done on Wednesday morning by one of the department's electronic analysts.

CHAPTER 6

THE FENCE

On Tuesday morning, shortly after nine-thirty, Sydney Malone entered Hunter Jewelry in Providence, and Garrett Hunter immediately smiled as she approached the counter.

"Well, good morning. Have you decided to take my offer? I now have the money in my safe," he asked.

"Considering that other jewelry stores wouldn't even consider paying cash for the pearls, I'll take you up on your offer. If I'm going to buy that furniture today, I need the cash. I'm sure you'll do quite well in reselling these. They clearly are worth far more than $5,000, we both know that."

"Ma'am, if you feel uncomfortable with what I'm offering, then by all means, don't take the offer. But, keep in mind that I never asked you for proof of ownership on the pearls, nor am I asking you for your name and address for my records. Perhaps this mutual agreement might lead to other items you might wish to sell in the future," Hunter answered.

Without replying, Sydney pulled out the necklace and ring from her bag, and laid it on the counter before Garrett. He quickly scanned the two items, and analyzed the necklace carefully. Within a few minutes, he was satisfied that the items were genuine and the same ones he had tested the day before. He excused himself to Sydney, and unlocked a door off the showroom floor that led to his office. The wall outside his office was equipped with a one-way glass window, which allowed him to view the showroom undetected from his office. He, too, had cameras mounted at several vantage points in the store, but they were hidden in ceiling vents, out of view of customers.

Before he opened the safe in his office, he glanced through the window as Sydney stood there with a nervous look on her face. Was she so obvious in the way she handled this situation that Garrett Hunter clearly was aware he was dealing with stolen property? *Sydney girl, you may be in over your head this time. Get the hell out of here and don't look back,* she thought.

"Here we are, ma'am, $5,000 in cash, as you requested. It's been a pleasure, and I do hope we can do more business together again soon."

Without so much as any direct eye contact between the two, Sydney took the money, quickly placed it in her bag, and headed for the door as she replied, "Have a good day." She walked briskly down Dorrance Street, and in a few minutes entered the Providence Public Library and climbed the stairs to the second floor reference room. She grabbed a newspaper from the rack, and sat down as if she was about to read it. All the while, she never read a word as she regained her composure, and felt assured that no one had followed her in. Ten minutes later, she left by another exit on the Atwells Avenue side just to be certain. She crossed the street and entered the parking garage adjacent to the Holiday Inn, and entered her 2011 Toyota RAV4. She looked all around her, and took off her blonde wig and sunglasses, and drove out the exit undetected, sporting short black hair as she left. This had been her biggest payday yet.

* * *

Drew Diamond had lived only a short while in his apartment in Lincoln, Rhode Island. Following his wife's sudden death in an auto accident a few years earlier on Route 146, when her car skidded on ice into a guard rail, and she had flown through the windshield into the path of an oncoming vehicle across the median, Drew had been devastated. He had been looking forward to his upcoming retirement from the police force just a few months later. It was ironic that, while he ran the risk of dying from heart failure or in the line of duty, it was his wife who died, crushing his dreams of happy retirement years together.

When he accepted the investigator's position at Assurance, the commute from his home on Salisbury Street in Worcester, Massachusetts to the Assurance office in Lincoln, Rhode Island took about an hour each way during rush hour periods. He thought this to be too much time just to get to and from his new job every day, so he had sold his home of thirty years in favor of an apartment in the Kirkbriar Apartments in Lincoln, five minutes from Assurance. Unfortunately, the apartment complex had no garages, just parking spaces outside each apartment, which meant he often needed to scrape the frost off from his windshield or snow from any snowfall, a chore he could do without.

Drew also disliked the barking dog he could hear from the apartment next door, a small cocker spaniel that was the loving companion of a sweet eighty-year old spinster. Rather than complain to the landlord about the noise from the dog, or her TV blaring until eleven every night, he decided not to renew his lease and look for a condo where no dogs were allowed, or where the barrier between condos was a common garage area rather than abutting living rooms. All he needed was a one- or two-bedroom unit with a garage, and there were several condo developments within a few miles from Assurance that looked appealing. Larchwoods in North Smithfield was one, and Brimfield Common in Cumberland was another. Both had available units for sale, and Drew set up appointments to see both of them.

Larchwoods' development had a hundred units ranging from one-bedroom to three-bedroom units, and its location was quite isolated from much traffic. After walking through one of the units, he was not convinced the condo complex was near enough to banks, shopping areas, and restaurants. Although he was seeking more peace and quiet within his own unit, he appreciated being near other convenient amenities the area had to offer. But he kept an open mind as he scheduled a viewing of a unit at Brimfield Common in Cumberland at five o'clock that Tuesday afternoon after he left the Attleboro police station.

The agent representing the owner of Unit 335 on Brimfield Drive greeted Drew as he approached the front door of the unit.

"You must be Mr. Diamond. I'm pleased to meet you. My name is Sydney, Sydney Malone. Shall we go in?" she asked.

"Please call me Drew, everyone does. Mr. Diamond sounds too rich for me, no pun intended," he replied.

"Okay, Drew, this unit has two bedrooms. There is a master bedroom with its own full bathroom, and a second bedroom, which you could turn into a den or an office, if you like. The second bathroom is just off the second bedroom, and is the one most guests would use, if and when you entertain. As you can see, the kitchen and great room have an open space concept with a gas-operated fireplace. Beyond the kitchen, there is a utility closet for a washer and dryer, and a second closet for storage. That area leads directly to the one-car garage in the back of the unit. Everything is on one level, and the unit has a full basement for storage, or it can be converted into another den or office area, if you like."

Drew remarked, "Hardwood floors in the open area, and granite counters in the kitchen, including on the island in the kitchen, this has a nice touch. I like the layout. I live at Kirkbriar Apartments now, and the closest bank and shopping areas are at the Lincoln Mall, a few miles down the Washington Highway. I'm not too familiar with this area. What are we talking about for things around this area, Sydney?"

"Banks, food markets, restaurants, churches, are all within a mile. The Washington Highway is about five minutes from here. And although these units aren't strictly for people over fifty-five, there are few children in the development, and the common wall between units is against the den or second bedroom, very quiet and double-insulated so you don't hear anything," she replied.

"Do I look like I'm over fifty-five?" he asked.

"Quite the contrary, Drew, I'd guess you were in your forties, not that my opinion really means much," she answered.

"Listen, Sydney, I'm very interested in this place, but there's so much more I need to know, and it's getting close to six o'clock. Can I interest you in talking more about the unit over dinner at one of the restaurants nearby? If I'm being too bold, I'll back off, but it's a quick way for me to familiarize myself with the surroundings."

"Well, that's a bit unusual, but I've got no one to go home to, and I'd rather go to a restaurant than have to cook when I get home. You're not going to jump over the table at the restaurant and attack me or anything like that, are you?" she asked with a smile on her face.

Drew could not believe he had just been so outspoken with this extraordinarily beautiful woman, imposing himself to her out of the blue. Since his wife had died a few years earlier, he had not dated any women at all. At fifty-six, he was flattered that she thought him to be much younger. Since he had begun to work at Assurance, his waistline had dropped in conjunction with better eating habits, and as a result, his heart was in good shape. He had decided to end his life of solitude, and wanted to socialize once more. Living as a widower was boring and depressive, and he had mourned his wife's death long enough. It was time to break out of his shell.

"Strictly business, I promise. If everything works out, I might be ready to make this happen."

Sydney walked to her car and watched as Drew's Lexus 350 SUV pulled up behind her. She led the way to Angelo's, an Italian restaurant about a mile up the road from the condominium complex. It was a Tuesday evening, and the restaurant was not too crowded, and they were immediately seated.

"Do you like wine, Sydney? Perhaps we can share a bottle of red or white?" he asked even before a waitress appeared with menus.

"A nice cabernet would be fine," she answered.

The waitress arrived, took their drink order, and returned shortly with a mid-priced cabernet and two wine goblets.

"So how long have you been with Morgan Realty group?"

"Believe it or not, it's been nearly ten years now. When my husband died, we didn't have much money. We'd only been married a few years, so I needed a job, and real estate sounded like fun. There have been some up and down years, and the downers make you realize not to spend it all during the good years. Let's just say I haven't hit the mother lode yet in this business, but I'm working on it."

"I'm sorry to hear about your husband. How did he die? He must have been young."

"Afghanistan, 2009. He was twenty-two, a Marine. He stepped on a landmine and died instantly."

"And you haven't remarried after all these years? There must be someone special who's come along by now?"

She bowed her head down for what seemed five minutes to Drew, all the while not saying a word. She then quickly lifted her face and stared at Drew.

"I thought you said this was going to be strictly business...the condo unit remember?" she asked.

"You are correct. Forgive me. Let's order, and while we wait for dinner, we can talk about real estate taxes, condo fees, and all that other good stuff."

As the evening progressed, and answers to all his questions were satisfied, they set a date for him to visit the Morgan Realty Group office on Diamond Hill Road on Wednesday.

"You've even named a street with my name on it," he quipped as he insisted on paying for dinner before they left. Although she argued that it was a business expense for her, he replied that it was a pleasure and it was his idea to have dinner in the first place.

She never asked him what he did for a living.

CHAPTER 7

RICHIE

Richie Volpe was a thirty-two-year-old thug whose life on Federal Hill in Providence had been filled with one crime after another. At age thirteen, he was sent to reform school in Cranston, Rhode Island for stealing forty bicycles, repainting them, and then selling them for fifty dollars each after inserting flyers in every mailbox on Federal Hill. The only reason he had been caught was because the father of one of the victims had carved his name on a metal plate under the bicycle seat, and Richie never noticed it. When the father showed up to buy another bicycle for his son at Richie's sale location, he saw a bike model just like the one he had originally bought for his son. Call it intuition, but the father casually looked under the seat as he was inspecting the bike, and saw the name plate. He called the police, and after they arrived and searched the garage Richie was using for the sale, they uncovered several cans of paint in different colors and an assortment of different types of bicycle locks.

After spending three months in confinement doing community work, like highway trash pickup, and mowing highway median areas in 2002, he was released and returned home. He lived with his mother in a third floor apartment on Vinton Street, off Atwells Avenue near the Italian restaurant strip known as DePasquale Square. Richie's father had abandoned the mother when Richie was only four, and she struggled to make ends meet. From seven in the morning to three in the afternoon, she worked at the Quality Diner on Weybosset Street. She would always be at Richie's school to pick him up, but by six in the evening, immediately following dinner, she would get a sitter to care for him until she returned from her waitress job at Camille's Roman Garden around eleven. This is where she met Bruno Gambardella, the new capo, the captain in the mafia Santucci family.

Gambardella had inquired about her one night while he was dining at Camille's with another woman companion. He could see how hard she worked and had been told she was a single mother raising her son, and barely surviving. When she waited on his table, he always gave her a very generous tip, and once told her that her son could work for him when he was old enough, if that would help them out.

As Richie reached ten and eleven years old, his mother relied less on babysitters, believing Richie was capable of staying home by himself until she got home. Often, when she returned home at night, he was sound asleep with the television on. However, as time passed, Richie became restless at home by himself, and started hanging out with other street kids, not exactly an awe-inspiring character builder in those circles. Fortunately, he evaded the police when a break-in or shoplifting incident nearly got him back in jail. Rona Volpe decided it was time to take Bruno Gambardella up on his offer to put Richie to work for him. So Richie became an errand boy to not only Bruno, but other members of the Santucci family.

Sitting in the office of his boss, Raymond Santucci, head of the family, Richie was still collecting money for someone else. If it wasn't from the bookmaking business, it was from the protection business. So the extra money he received from fencing stolen jewelry at Hunter's Jewelry was a main source of his income. The rest came from his take on the collection money he picked up every week from the thirty businesses he was responsible for handling.

He wanted out of the life of crime. His mother, now in her fifties and showing all those years on her feet at two jobs each day, walked with constant aches in her knees. The doctors at the Urgent Care Clinic on Broad Street had indicated to her that X-rays showed badly torn cartilage in both knees, and that knee replacements were recommended. She could not wait on tables any longer at Camille's, and fortunately, the diner she worked in had her running the cash register, sitting down behind a counter.

What does a thirty-two-year-old uneducated thug with little or no experience in any field do to make a decent living? How would he start a new life outside of crime, and build a career in some good paying field which would enable him to raise a family of his own?

"You're asking me for advice? You people who force me to pay you $200 a week for protection, you want to know how to stop being a criminal?" asked Garrett Hunter with a bewildered look on his face as Richie Volpe posed the question to him.

"Look, Garrett, I don't like it any more than you do," answered Volpe, "but I do what I'm told or I'm in big trouble. And, if I'm in trouble, you're in trouble."

"Richie, I can buy insurance for protection from business interruption from any insurance company in the business, and for a hell of a lot less than $10,000 a year, so don't go around thinking you're doing me a favor. But I don't want any trouble, so I pay it. Tell me, how do you tell your boss you suddenly want to get out? It can't be that easy. Won't he make you an offer you can't refuse, or you'll find a horse's head at the foot of your bed one morning?"

"It's not like that at all anymore. I'm not involved in anything but collections, and I don't want to know what else goes on at the Ocean State Olive Oil Company. I'm just a gofer, and I'm tired of doing this to honest businessmen like you. I got nothing, Garrett, and I'm going nowhere if I keep doing this. If I had $200 a week to pass along to the capo, I'd do it myself. I'm not kidding. I was just hoping you had some suggestions I could look into."

Garrett looked at Richie, and genuinely felt sorry for him. Here stood a tough guy who didn't want to be tough anymore, and he had never thought about what else he could do to make a living, other than a life of crime.

"Sometimes you have to work smarter, not harder. I put in a lot of hours in the jewelry business, but the products I sell do most of the work. People know gold, silver, diamonds, and other precious metals are expensive. I buy wholesale and wait for someone to come in and pay retail. I'm not building a wall or rewiring a house or fixing your toilets to get paid. I get paid to wait. Once you know your business, and I've studied a long time at knowing mine, other people who buy from you will make you richer. Just ask your boss why he charges little guys like me? It's because he doesn't lift a finger to get that money. Do you understand what I'm trying to tell you?"

"Yea, but what do I know about jewelry?"

"It doesn't have to be about jewelry. It can be about buying and selling securities with other people's money, selling people's houses for a commission in the real estate business. You don't need to get into a trade unless that's what you want, and you think you can be good at it. And don't confuse my success with being an honest businessman. I've fenced some of your stuff a few times. That's illegal, but the stuff was probably insured by whoever it was stolen from, so I don't feel too bad about it. Nobody got hurt, and I didn't break any kneecaps along the way. It's not the same as stealing the purse off a little old lady. That is just not good, it's mean, Richie, and what you do right now is mean. Suppose I suddenly refuse to pay anymore? Will there be a sudden fire in my store one night, or somebody harassing my kids?"

"I'm not like that, Garrett. I've never hurt anyone yet."

"That's probably because no one has ever refused to pay. They're afraid of what might happen if they did. What would you do to me if your boss wanted you to show me a lesson because I wouldn't keep paying?"

"That's why I don't want to do this anymore. I don't want that day to happen, because I'm afraid of what he'd want me to do."

"Okay, here's what you need to do. Tell your mother the two of you are moving to Florida by June, five months from now. The warmer weather will be good for her, and it's a lot cheaper to live down there. If that doesn't suit her, get her to move outside this area. You've got to get out of this area because Gambardella will always know you're around, and you'll never be rid of him. You have to convince your mother that you both have to get out of Rhode Island, the further away the better. If you truly did only a collector's job, he can easily get someone to take that over. But I wouldn't want to bump into him from time to time to remind him you're still around, and that you may know too much. Do you understand me?"

"But wherever I go, I need to make enough money to support my mom and I. Where do I start?"

"I may have a pretty good fence customer in the coming weeks, and I could use someone to unload the stuff in New York. It's not really legal, but it will give you some pretty good money until you qualify for something legitimate. In order for you to sell real estate, for example, you need to get a license, and you have to pass some tests first before you can sell. The same would apply to buying and selling securities. For that matter, you'll need to be trained for any job you get. That will take months to happen. But, heck, you can't reach for the stars just yet, it will take time."

"Selling houses sounds like it could be real profitable, and I don't need to spend a lot of money to do it. But first, I've got to come up with some excuse for Bruno that will get me out of the collection business. Then I can take some real estate courses at the Real Estate Institute of Rhode Island in Warwick. I was on the computer last night, and the tuition is only $325, and I can work for you while I'm taking the courses. Who's this fence you're dealing with anyway?"

"It's better that you don't know. Nothing may come of it, but the fence might have a lot of steady jewelry coming my way in the next few weeks. I'm not sure yet, but I've got two pieces you could take to New York for me now. Once my contacts see the product, they'll call me to make an offer. If I accept, they'll give you a sealed suitcase with a combination lock on it. I'm the only one who has the combination, and they will lock it after putting my money in it. When you get back, I'll tell you where we can meet. Once I count the money to make certain they haven't screwed me, I'll call you to get your cut."

"What are we talking about here?" Richie asked.

"Somewhere around $5,000 or more. That should hold you for a while, but you can't keep going with these collections for Gambardella. It will be better if you're not in my store again, you understand? If I see a new face next week in here to collect the $200, I'll know you've had the talk with him. Leave me a phone number where I can reach you. And by the way, forget about taking a real estate course in Warwick. Didn't you hear me when I told you that you've got to get out of Rhode Island?"

"Why are you doing this, Garrett? Nobody's ever done anything for me before."

"Someday, you might be in a position to help someone else out, Richie. You'll know when it happens, it will just feel right. This feels right for me right now, and if I can do it, why not? But get out of Providence. I don't care if it's Massachusetts or Connecticut, but find some place where you and your mother are out of sight. Rhode Island is just too small to try to stay out of sight. It may not be as easy as you think to just walk away. I don't trust these people."

CHAPTER 8

THE UNEXPECTED

Mary Donovan's family had owned a crude retreat home deep in the heart of the Great North Woods in Pittsburg, New Hampshire since 1925. When her father died in 1990, the property was passed on to her. Mary had been married to Drew Diamond at the time, and when she died in 2016, the property was willed to Drew. He and Mary had gone there with their two children only twice in all those years, but the house had been rented each year during hunting season, and a maintenance service cleaned the cabin monthly in exchange for keeping any rental money they could get from campers during the summer months. The maintenance service would inform Drew of any repairs that were needed, and Drew Junior would go up to the house with some college buddies to make sure the log cabin was in good condition once the repairs were completed.

The log cabin had three rooms, a large living area with a stone fireplace on one end of the room, and a small wood-burning stove on the other end near the kitchen area. The wooden kitchen table had four matching chairs, and the kitchen range was operated by oil, and also provided heat when not in use for cooking. There was a sink in the kitchen with a hand pump that provided water from a well. Hot water for baths was provided by a huge kettle on the stove. Off the kitchen were two bedrooms with wall-to-wall carpeting and well-insulated paneled walls. Adjacent to the bedrooms was a small room that contained a bathtub and nothing else. This room had been designated as the future bathroom at one time. Electric lights and plugs were installed throughout the cabin, but only worked with a generator as there was no other access to electricity this deep in the woods.

When Mary first inherited the property, she had told Drew that the only way she would ever spend time there was if they installed some inside bathroom facility. In 1992, Drew had gone up to the house with a few friends to install a septic tank for a toilet, and a sink for washing up. On the roof of the house, they constructed a platform that would hold a two hundred seventy-five gallon tank directly over the sink and toilet below. The system was crude at best, but the bathroom was functional, enough to get Mary to agree to spend a week there with the family.

* * *

After leaving the restaurant and the meeting with Sydney Malone, Drew drove back to his apartment. As he poured himself an amaretto on ice, a smile came across his face as he remembered the New Hampshire house's bathroom facilities when compared to the elaborate bathroom in the condo he had just visited. Then the smile turned into sadness as he thought about Mary.

How he missed her. It wasn't supposed to be like this.

He picked up his smart phone and punched in his son's number and heard the phone ringing on the other end.

"Hi, this is Drew."

"Junior, it's Dad. Guess what, I think I'm buying a new place, a two-bedroom condo in Cumberland. It's only about ten minutes from Assurance, and it's got a garage. My lease runs out next month over here at Kirkbriar, and this new place is all on one level to boot. Are you available this weekend? I can give you a tour. Maybe Claire can come down with you, and we can all go to dinner afterwards?" he asked. "The drive back to Narragansett shouldn't be too bad after dinner."

"Claire has to be at the Marriott in Providence on Saturday for a seminar for prospective real estate agents, and I'm downtown too on Saturday, getting ready for a big commercial closing on Monday. We were going to grab dinner at The Capitol Grille, but this sounds better. I'll check with Claire tomorrow just to be sure, but for now it's a go," he answered.

Claire O'Brien was a twenty-five year old realtor in Narragansett, born and raised in the South County area of Rhode Island. Drew Jr. had met her at a closing of a commercial business in Wakefield two years earlier. He was impressed with her efficiency in completing the transaction, and boldly asked if she would join him for dinner that evening to celebrate. The attraction to each other was apparent, and she accepted without hesitation. Over the following two years, they had grown much closer, and Junior popped the question to her at Christmastime. Their wedding was planned for June of the current year.

Claire had inherited the realty business from her father. He and Claire's mother had perished in 2015 when their Delta Airlines flight from Rome to Boston had crashed in the Atlantic, fifteen-hundred miles from the U.S. coast. There had been no survivors. Claire was a recent graduate from the University of Rhode Island in Kingston at age twenty-one at the time.

She had recently started her career in her father's office when the tragedy occurred. There were six agents in the office, all of them with far more experience than she had. For her to suddenly assume leadership of the agency, that required a special skill in spite of numerous hurdles. But she clearly was up to the task as she spent nearly sixty hours a week in the business.

Junior, now a third-year associate with Smalley & Sons, also spent considerable time in real estate law, and was a favorite of the real estate partner in this twelve-law-yer firm. The few hours he spent with Claire each week were very precious, and even then, it was not unusual to see both of them with their heads buried in work from their offices when they had a moment.

The plan was for Drew to go to Sydney's office in Smithfield where they would review the details of the asking price, and if they could agree on a final price, Drew would make a ten percent deposit and the balance at the closing a few weeks later. He arrived at her office on Thursday morning at nine. Sydney was expecting him, and was all smiles when he arrived. She was as lovely as the day before, and Drew's warm handshake made her blush, an obvious gesture that did not go unnoticed by Drew.

"First of all, Drew, thank you for dinner the other night. You mentioned the death of my husband at dinner, and I was a bit curt in my reply, and I'm sorry for that. You were just being kind. I think it's finally time for me to move on with my life. I don't have dinner with any men all that often, other than with my boss, the manager of the agency, and he's a very happily married man."

"You don't need to apologize to me for anything. We had set the ground rules for dinner, and I overstepped them at the restaurant. I'm the one who should be apologizing."

"Since his funeral nearly eleven years ago now, I've hesitated to do much socializing, spending most of my time in real estate. You're the first person to ask about him in years. It's time I get my life back. My seclusion won't get him back."

"I've been there, Sydney. I lost my wife two years ago in a freak car accident after just retiring from the Worcester police force. I thought we'd be spending the next thirty years enjoying retirement, but somebody had other plans," he stated as if he suddenly was far away.

"Anyway, I'm really interested in the condo at Brimfield Common, and I'm ready to make an offer on the property for just $10,000 less than what they want. The carpets are pretty worn out, and I'll probably have the rooms painted before I move in. If the owner agrees, I'm ready to do the deal. There's no mortgage to worry about, so we can close pretty fast."

"Let me call the owner today, and if she agrees, I'll draw up the purchase and sale agreement. The woman who had the condo died a few months ago, and it's her daughter who's handling the sale."

"If she agrees with my offer, do you think I could show the place late Saturday afternoon to my son and his fiancé? I'd like them to see where I'm going to live."

"Well, I can't let you go in there by yourselves until the closing occurs, but I don't have another appointment on Saturday after three, so I can be there. Just let me know the time you expect to be there."

On Friday night, the RAV4 was parked three hundred yards from the house at 22 Sycamore Lane in Pawtucket, Rhode Island. As Sydney looked at her watch, the residents of the house entered their car, and a few minutes later, at seven o'clock, drove past her car. It was overcast and pitch dark as she drove the RAV just beyond the driveway with its lights out, and turned off the motor. She then quickly made her way to the rear of the house, where there were two cellar windows. She tried the first one, but it would not budge. She then moved to the other window and that one she was able to push open.

As she slid her way through the small window opening and relocked the cellar window, she turned her flashlight on as she made her way up the stairs to a door leading into the kitchen. She could see a lamp in the living room corner that was turned on, so she turned off her flashlight. She quietly began to walk toward a bedroom, where she normally had most of her success in previous break-ins.

Suddenly, out of the living room, she heard the loud growling of a dog.

"Oh, crap. They've got a dog," she whispered.

She quickly reached in her pocket for a handful of crackers and some sugar cubes, and she carefully placed them on the floor in front of her. The German shepherd welcomed the treats and immediately quieted down. Sydney continued into the bedroom and began searching through every drawer in the room, gathering jewelry that was hidden in a drawer, again ignoring a box that sat on the counter of a dresser, and another atop an armoire. But none of the drawers contained any cash.

The dog wanted more, and started following Sydney from room to room, which began to irritate her as the shepherd kept poking her from behind. She jerked away from the dog, and looked for the rear door. Once she saw the door, she bolted for it. The dog ran after her and lunged at her pants leg, ripped the pants, and appeared to penetrate the skin at the back of her right leg. She turned and kicked the dog away as she frantically fumbled the lock on the rear door and managed to quickly close the door behind her. The dog was barking loudly as Sydney hobbled toward her car, holding her hand tightly against her ripped pants. The leg felt like it was on fire as she grimaced while entering the car.

She looked at her hand, and there was no blood, though she found this hard to believe because of the pain shooting up her leg. As she started the engine, she could feel the torn spandex area, and she cringed as she drove rapidly away, the sack of jewelry tossed on the passenger side of the car. Within minutes, she crossed into Attleboro and then Cumberland. The fifteen minute ride to her one-bedroom apartment on Mendon Road in Cumberland seemed like an eternity. She took the elevator to the fifth floor, and rushed to enter her apartment. Fortunately for her, no one saw her enter, still all dressed in black and wearing black sneakers.

She rushed to the bathroom and stripped off the spandex leggings and grabbed the hand mirror. She could see a black and blue mark on the back of her leg the size of a silver dollar. She quickly applied triple antibiotic ointment to the wound, and then slipped on a pair of jeans, ever so slowly. She grabbed the torn spandex leggings, put on her coat, and headed down the elevator back to her car. On the ground level of the apartment building, she tossed the spandex into a trash bin and drove a mile away to the Urgent Care clinic.

It was now eight o'clock, and the clinic was virtually empty. The receptionist could see that Sydney was in pain, and immediately called one of the doctors on duty.

"So, you have a dog bite. Let's take a look," the doctor said.

"I was just taking a walk near my apartment about an hour ago, and this German shepherd came out of a wooded area near the sidewalk and lunged at me from behind. He had a leash, so he must have gotten away from his owner. I don't know who he belongs to, but he took a chunk of my pants and hit the skin," she said as she brought her jeans down to reveal the bruise.

"That's quite a hematoma you've got there, Miss. I doubt the dog had rabies if he was on a leash, but you can never be sure. I'll have to give you a tetanus shot. It looks like you've put some sort of ointment on it."

"Just some triple antibiotic cream I had. That's when I realized I'd better get this checked."

"I'm also going to prescribe some antibiotic tablets for a couple of days just to be safe. You'll likely be sore for a few days, so try not to place too much weight on the leg for a while."

On Saturday morning, she called Drew Diamond to inform him she would be at the condo by five-thirty. The daughter of the late owner had accepted his offer and Drew was in a very good mood.

"Sydney, you will come out to dinner afterwards won't you? I'd like you to celebrate my new home with me and the kids," he asked.

"I'll probably take a rain check on that. I'm nursing a dog bite injury on the back of my leg, and I don't think I'll be good company."

"Are you sure you want us to do this today? We can reschedule if you're not up to it."

"No, it's just a bruise. I had it treated at Urgent Care. I just don't think I'd be good company for dinner after the tour. I may not find a comfortable spot to sit at the restaurant."

"Maybe you'll change your mind by the end of the day. And if you're still hurting, hopefully there will be another day."

Sydney walked gingerly through the three house showings on Saturday morning and early afternoon. The soreness at the back of her leg seemed to be less painful than the night before when she laid awake most of the night. Obviously, the painkillers were working, although she hesitated to take any more than she had to. Perhaps dinner out wouldn't be such a bad idea. The thought of having to make her own dinner almost never appealed to her, and celebrating a sale was always a good excuse.

She arrived at the condo at five o'clock, sensing that Drew and his guests would be earlier than expected. Her premonition proved to be correct as the doorbell to the condo rang and Drew entered, followed by Junior and Claire at five-thirty.

"Sydney, this is my son, Drew Junior, and his fiancée, Claire O'Brien. They're in real estate, too. Drew is a real estate lawyer in Providence, and Claire has her own agency in Narragansett."

"Oh, hi, I know Claire. I've been to one of her seminars in the past," Sydney said as she shook their hands.

Drew could not wait to show them all the qualities of his new home. They, in turn, loved the layout, the proximity to shopping and banking nearby, and the apparent serenity off the back deck, which faced an environmental preserve. While the garage was adjacent to the next unit's garage, the only wall common to both units was off the guest bedroom. To Drew, this meant not having to listen to the annoying barking of a next door dog, a nightly event he could do without.

"You seem to be moving around without too much difficulty, Sydney. Is that dog bite still bothering you?" he asked.

"Actually, I'm feeling pretty good right now. Pain-killers help, but with my pants on, you'd never know I've been bitten by a dog in the last day," she responded with a smirk on her face as she smiled Drew's way.

"Does that mean you'll join us for dinner?"

"Your friendly agent would be delighted to join you, but if I flinch a few times in my seat, just ignore me."

In the meantime, the owners of 22 Sycamore Lane in Pawtucket had reported a break-in at their home on Friday evening. The woman had filed a report of missing jewelry worth several thousand dollars. When the police arrived, they found pieces of dog food on the bedroom carpet, along with a swatch of black spandex. The rear door was unlocked, and a drawer in the bedroom was left open.

"Looks like your visitor left early. Everything in your home is in place, except for that one open drawer. A messy intruder would not care how disheveled he left the inside of the house. This looks very much like the same person who's been breaking in at several other homes in the area over the last month. But I suspect your dog was more than he bargained for."

"That's not all he missed, Officer. We have video cameras at the rear of the property. They get triggered by any movement in the yard, and the footage runs for about

two minutes before it stops, unless there is more movement. We have two sets of movement, the first at five after
seven, and the other at seven fifteen on Friday night. The
guy can be seen entering the cellar window. He must be a
little guy, but we can't make out his face. It was too dark.
The second clip shows him running out of the yard a few
minutes later, holding the back of his right leg."

"We'll need that tape, ma'am. Maybe our tech guy
at the station can make this clearer in spite of the dark
background. I'm always amazed at what they can do with
videos."

Unfortunately, later on Saturday, the tech clerk was
unable to make any headway with the recording. All he
could detect was that the subject was around five-feet six
inches tall and weighed about a hundred pounds. The
black hat and gloves worn by the intruder made it impossible to identify any distinguishable features on the dark
image.

"It's a longshot," the patrolman said, "but if it really
was a dog bite on the burglar's right leg, maybe it was
treated at a hospital by a doctor. I guess if it happened
to me, I'd go to an urgent care facility or the emergency
room of a hospital to get them to look at it."

On Sunday morning at ten o'clock, there was a knock
on Sydney's apartment door. She was still in her robe
nursing a coffee, and reading the Sunday morning newspaper. She looked through the peephole in her door, and
did not recognize the police officer standing there.

"Who is it, please?" she asked cautiously as she made
sure her deadbolt lock was on.

"Sergeant Peterson of the Cumberland Police, ma'am. I'm just following up on your recent visit to Urgent Care on Friday night," the policeman stated as he clearly exposed his uniform and badge. "May I come in for a moment?"

She unlocked the door and slowly opened it. She was puzzled by the early call.

"What can I do for you, Officer?"

"You were treated for a dog bite late Friday evening. Hopefully, that's not too serious. But a loose dog running without its owner is a violation of a town ordinance, and a danger to pedestrians, ma'am. And I was wondering what you can tell me about the incident."

"Well, there's not much to tell. I went out about seven for a walk, now that the sidewalks are clear of any snow, and while I was walking on Mendon Road, this dog came out of nowhere and lunged at me from behind, and took a chunk of my leggings in the back of my right leg. I turned around, and the dog just took off. I'm not sure what kind of dog it was, maybe a German shepherd. It was too dark to make it out, but I could see a reflection from some metal on the dog's leash. It had to have broken away from its owner. I wasn't too far from the Chimney Hill Apartment complex, if that helps," Sydney related.

"Are you okay? The Urgent Care notified us about the dog bite. Any time someone gets treated for something that might be the result of an unwarranted attack or assault, they have to report it to us. Sometimes it's a domestic issue, sometimes it's someone getting assaulted walking alone at night. We can't have dogs running around loose, but I guess you know why by now."

"They gave me a shot, and told me to stay off my feet for a few days. It's sore, but I'll survive. I'm impressed though, you guys following up on a dog bite."

"Well, we wouldn't want it happening again to someone else if we can prevent it, would we? Thank you for your time, ma'am. You have a good day," the policeman said as he left the apartment.

Sydney just breathed a sigh after he left.

CHAPTER 9

THE DISAPPEARANCE

The following Monday, Richie Volpe showed up at Hunter Jewelry. Garrett Hunter was disappointed. He had expected to make his protection payment to someone else.

"So, I take it your conversation with Gambardella didn't go over so well?"

"I'm not sure how it went. The capo said he would get back to me with an answer sometime this week. He said there were a few things he needed to do before he let me go. He was very sympathetic about my mom's knees, and he remembered her when she worked at Camille's. It's not as if I took a code or anything, Garrett. I'm just a gofer, and I've never been in on any conversations directly related to the family, never."

"That's not a clean break, Richie. If they give you the okay, I'd get the hell out of here with your mother real fast. Go to Maine or New Hampshire. Try to find a small town for now, and pay everything by cash. No college town or ocean resort either. When you're settled, call me and I'll get you started going to New York for me," Garrett added.

"Don't call me and give your name. Say it's Waldo calling and leave a cell phone number, or even better, get a smart phone and I can text you without talking to you."

"You really think they won't just let me leave without any trouble, do you?"

"Smarten up, Richie. This isn't your local choir group telling you it's okay to drop out of the choir because you have laryngitis. Some of your colleagues in the past have been known to disappear. What little you say you know, in their minds might still be too much. Go while you can. Here's two thousand dollars to get you going. I'd give you more, but it's Monday and I don't keep that much cash in the store unless I know I'll need it. You can pay me back from some of the money you'll make working for me in a couple of weeks or so. If I don't get a call from you by next Saturday, you probably didn't make it. For your mother's sake, I hope I get the call."

"Why are you doing this? I asked you that before. You don't owe me anything, quite the contrary. You should hate my guts for hustling you every week. Nobody's ever given a crap about me, except my mother."

"Because I've been there. Maybe not with the mob, but five years in the state pen at Norfolk for stealing cars when I was twenty years old. My father owned this store before me, but it was in Warwick at the Rhode Island Mall then. Once the Warwick Mall opened next door, the lower traffic made him decide to move to Providence. He retired last year, and I pay him every month. He holds the mortgage on this building, and my monthly check to him covers the mortgage and some for him to live on in Florida with my mother. Five years from now, the mortgage will be paid and this building will be mine. I would have kept on stealing cars or worse if my father hadn't taught me the jewelry business. Pay it forward, Richie. Someday you might be in a position to do the same for someone else."

Tears welled in Richie's eyes as he hugged Garrett, and then turned away and headed out the door.

"I'll take this week's two hundred out of the money you just gave me. I hope I don't see you next week, but I hope to be talking to you soon."

* * *

Bruno Gambardella had taken Richie under his wing years earlier when he had noticed his mother working at two jobs to feed and clothe him. He remembered a similar background when years gone by Raymond Santucci had taken him in when he was just nineteen. Now at the age of fifty, Gambardella stood as Santucci's capo, his top lieutenant and most trusted advisor. He was capable of handling any and all affairs for Santucci, who was approaching seventy years old, and ready to hand over the family to Bruno.

So, how to deal with Richie's request to get out of the collection and bookmaking business was strictly Bruno's decision, and no one else. He called Richie into his office and told him to close the door before he sat down.

"Let's talk about you leaving the family. What do you know about the businesses we're in?"

"Bruno, all I know are the twenty stores I collect from each week and the guys who carry our betting cards. I don't know anything about any other businesses you're in, and I don't really want to know. I've got a little money saved, and I want to take my mom where it's warmer. She's not well, Bruno. She has trouble walking, and this damn winter weather is only going to make it worse. I want to take her south, Florida, South Carolina, maybe even Arizona, someplace where she can recuperate from knee surgery, and not have to worry any more. I can find a job out there, and maybe meet a nice woman someday, and settle down, maybe raise a family of my own. My mom could spoil my kids. I've been loyal to you for years, and all I ask is to take my mom away with me so I can make her better, and she doesn't need to work anymore. I want to have a straight life. I just don't want to do this for the rest of my life."

"Your mother was very thankful years ago when I took you in. I remember how hard she worked, Richie. Do you swear to me, after all these years, that you'll never rat on the family about anything you know?"

"I've got nothing to say about anything in the family because all I know is my collections and my betting spots. If I knew anything more, I'd never talk about it. But I honestly only know what I do, nothing else. You've been good to me, Bruno."

"Okay, I believe you. When are you planning to make this move?"

"As soon as I can. The cold weather really bothers her now. Maybe in a couple of weeks from now. We'll drive down with a U-Haul trailer to South Carolina first, maybe Hilton Head, and see how that goes."

"One condition, once you're settled, let me know where you are. We should stay in touch," Gambardella said as he extended his outstretched hand to Richie, and gave him a firm handshake.

"Give my best to your mom, a wonderful woman."

At that moment, there were many feelings going through his mind. *Do I believe Bruno that it's okay to leave, and with his blessing?* It was too easy in Richie's mind, much too easy to suddenly just leave a family he had been associated with for over fifteen years. While Bruno could be caring and kind at times, Richie had witnessed his violent side at one time when one of his bookies was short in his collections two weeks in a row. He remembered how the bookie had been threatened by Bruno. And this was before Bruno had been elevated to capo by Santucci.

As he left Bruno's office and the Ocean State Olive Oil building, he cautiously walked to his car in the adjacent parking lot on the side of the building, glancing occasionally to be certain he was not being followed. He quickly drove toward his apartment on Vinton Street, removed a vent in his bedroom wall, and pulled out an envelope filled with cash. He then grabbed two suitcases from a hallway closet and emptied the drawers in his mother's dresser, cramming the clothes as best he could. He then reached for a grocery shopping bag and threw in her shoes and slippers. Every few minutes, he looked out the apartment window facing the street to see if anyone approached the building. No one approached.

He quickly ran down the back staircase of the apartment house and placed the suitcases inside the back door on the main level. In the next minute, he entered his car and drove around the block, parking his car on the next street in front of the house abutting the rear of his apartment building. He rushed through the back yard of the house and grabbed the suitcases and the bag of shoes. Suddenly, he heard the slamming of two car doors and he glanced around the corner of the house and saw two of Gambardella's men get out of their car and walk toward the front entrance to the building.

Richie hurried back to his car, tossed the suitcases in his trunk, and drove off toward the Quality Diner on Weybosset Street.

"Mom, I need you to come with me right now," he frantically called out to his mother.

"Richie, what are you doing here? I can't just leave my job right in the middle of the morning. What's so important?" she asked.

"Mom, if you want to see me alive for another day, you will come with me now, do you understand? I think Bruno's put a hit on me. I'll explain later, but please, you've got to come now."

"What are you talking about? You're scaring me right now, Richie."

"Mom, it's now or never, we need to go," he pleaded with his mother.

Rona Volpe had much difficulty in moving fast, and

it took her nearly five minutes just to put on her winter coat, grab her cane, and head for the back door through the kitchen of the restaurant. She told her boss in the kitchen that she would be right back. Richie carefully looked outside and no one was in sight. He had left the motor of his car running as he helped his mother into the front seat. As he exited the rear of the diner, he hesitated a second to be certain no one was following him. Rona was petrified as he quickly sped down Weybosset toward the entrance to Route 95 North between the Westin Hotel and the Providence Place Mall.

Once he passed Foxboro, Massachusetts, he had a choice to make. He could stay on Route 95 or take Route 495 toward New Hampshire. He opted for the Route 495 turnoff, preferring to avoid the Route 128 section of Route 95, which was always very congested.

"Okay, I'm calming myself down right now, and would you please tell me what the hell this is all about?" she asked.

"Mom, I decided to stop hustling money for Bruno, and I told him so this morning. He told me it was okay to leave, but I didn't trust him. He thinks I know too much, and he knows how to get rid of a problem. Even though I really don't know much about his other crooked dealings, he doesn't need to take that risk, certainly not from someone like me. He can simply make me disappear, and problem solved."

"Bruno wouldn't do that, Richie; he's taken care of you for years. Why would he stop now?"

"Because I don't want to do this anymore. I don't

want to be his errand boy. I want to own my own business someday and my own life and maybe my own kids if I can find a nice woman who'll marry a loser like me. When I was getting some of your clothes in suitcases, two of Bruno's guys pulled up in front of our house, Mom. I've never had anyone do that before, especially two guys I don't even deal with."

"So, where are we going?" Rona asked.

"As far away as we can from Providence for now. They think I'm taking you to South Carolina, so I don't expect them up north. It's not like I ratted on them and got away. But Bruno doesn't think like we do. He wants to eliminate a problem. That's me. Even though I don't know anything, he can't be sure about that. But I don't think he'll send anybody after me, I'm not that important."

Several hours later, they crossed Massachusetts into Portsmouth, New Hampshire, and then into Maine, where they stopped for lunch at Stonewall Kitchen in York. An hour later, they drove further north into Portland and checked in at the Embassy Suites by Hilton. The elevator took them to their third floor suite as he carried the two suitcases and Rona carried the bagful of footwear. He had checked in using the name Richard Lamb, and told the clerk he was paying cash for his two to three day stay.

Richie had a plan in place. He had arranged for a friend of his to rent a U-Haul truck locally in Providence that he could drive to a specific location in Kennebunk, Maine. He had given the friend a bill of sale for all the furniture in the apartment, showing that the friend had paid a thousand dollars for everything in the apartment.

If anyone questioned him about removing furniture from the apartment, he would flash the bill of sale, and tell them it was for his summer house in Plymouth, New Hampshire, which he legitimately owned. His wife would follow him up in their car. After leaving the van at the designated location, the friend and his wife would drive to their vacation home for the weekend.

In the late evening on Thursday, Richie would drive to Kennebunk, leave his car at the van's location, and drive the van to a storage facility nearby, where he would empty the van. He would then return the van to where his car was parked, and leave the empty vehicle there for the return trip to Providence on late Sunday afternoon. All the van rental papers were done in the friend's name. Richie had given his friend two hundred dollars to do this, and the friend swore he would not change his story when queried by anyone. Richie's drive from Portland to Kennebunk was only twenty-eight miles and took him just slightly over thirty minutes. When he returned to the suite, his mother was sound asleep in the bedroom with the TV still on.

So far his plan had been executed perfectly. Next came the task of finding a suitable apartment in Portland, and finding a job. Rona wanted to find something as well, but it needed to be a job where she could sit down to perform the job. Richie was reluctant to agree.

On Friday morning, he searched the classified ads in the *Portland Press Herald* newspaper, and circled several apartments that caught his eye. One rental ad, in particular, was for a four-room first floor apartment with two

bedrooms, a living room, and a large eat-in kitchen, including a refrigerator, stove, and microwave. The second
floor of the house was occupied by the owner and his
wife. They preferred the second floor because they had
a screened in porch in the rear of the apartment, with an
unobstructed view of the ocean. The owners had earlier
rented the first-floor unit to two college students going
to the University of Southern Maine, but that lasted only
until the Christmas break in December. The owners were
hoping to rent to older people who likely wouldn't create the kind of noise that the college students had creat-
ed. Richie liked the idea of his mom not having to climb
flights of stairs as she had done in Providence for years.

Richie and Rona drove to Sagamore Road, on the
outskirts of Portland, after calling to schedule a viewing
of the apartment. The owners were pleased to see a thirty-two-year-old man with his mother as the possible ten-
ants. The twelve month lease was acceptable to Richie,
and they made a payment for the first and last month of
the lease. The weekend would be dedicated to moving in,
a chore they actually looked forward to.

Next on the list was for Richie to secure a job. Any
job would do, so that he could immediately familiarize
himself with the area until more lucrative positions were
advertised. He returned to the classified ad pages once
they were settled in their new apartment.

CHAPTER 10

CAMERAS TELL A STORY

On the following Monday morning, Sydney walked into Hunter Jewelry wearing her long blonde wig and a long winter coat buttoned to the collar where a wool scarf wrapped around her neck. It was another bitterly cold winter day in Rhode Island. She removed her leather gloves and reached inside her shoulder bag as she approached Garrett Hunter at the counter.

"Welcome back, ma'am. It's a pleasure to see you again. What can I do for you on this chilly winter morning?" he asked.

"I have a few items you may be interested in," she answered as she laid the various jewelry pieces on the counter.

"Well, let's see here. The gold items I can probably have melted down, but the sapphire and ruby bracelets can probably be resold as is. As we discussed earlier, I am only too happy to take these off your hands, but you're free to go elsewhere if you feel the items are worth more than I can offer. Twelve hundred for the lot is all I can do."

"Are we talking twelve hundred in cash by tomorrow morning?"

"Of course, same terms as before," he replied.

"Then, I'll be back in the morning."

On Tuesday morning, Sydney followed the same routine as she had done the week before, entering the library for a few minutes, then exiting from a different door to a parking garage across the street, all the while making sure she was not being followed. Once she entered her car, she again glanced around the parking garage and removed the wig, placing it carefully in a hat box on the passenger seat as she drove away.

In the meantime, Drew Diamond sat at his desk at the Assurance office and reviewed the film footage once more from Simonton Jewelry. The video's quality was only fair at best, but the number of pixels made the film grainy. There were no clear images of the woman's face as she kept her head facing down toward the counter. The only time she lifted her head, she held her hand toward her mouth as if she was sniffing her own breath for some foul odor. She quickly grabbed the items on the counter, turned and exited the store.

Drew played and replayed the tape several times until, finally, he noticed a small tattoo on the blonde's neck, hardly visible at a distance from the camera. He zeroed in on the neck area, and following a few clicks from his video software, watched the area enlarge to twice its size, easily displaying a Purple Heart tattoo. He pressed the Print key on the photo and made a copy of the image. *Why would someone have a tattoo of a purple heart on their neck?* he asked himself. He then rewound the video on the tape to an area where the woman's entire body could be seen on the video as she entered the store. Again, with the manipulation of a few keys on his keyboard, Drew was able to get an estimate of the person's height...five feet six inches tall.

He checked his notes from the home security camera that had taken an image of a fleeing burglar with a dog bite, and saw that the estimate height of the burglar also was five feet six inches. Coincidence, perhaps, but Drew didn't think so.

"Well, well, do we have a female burglar here? I'll bet no one is thinking about a woman as the burglar."

The petite body necessary to enter through a cellar window was a given, but the thought of the intruder being a small woman would not be on anyone's radar, until now. Next, he reviewed the five oil servicemen who had serviced the homes of the victims in the last few months, and compiled a list of their names and addresses. He had a plan.

He would install several cameras in the basement of an Assurance associate's home, Art Donnelly, and would then call a serviceman to restart the furnace in that house. Donnelly would deliberately not remain in the basement, but would offer to be available to the repairman if he needed him. In the meantime, the associate would wait in the kitchen upstairs.

On Tuesday, Tom Holt from Superior Oil was the first to arrive. The house was a nine-room garrison with a circular drive in a beautiful development in Cumberland. Homes in this development all sold for more than $500,000. Once his work was done, Tom left the house. Drew sat in Donnelly's den reviewing the two monitors that pointed at the cellar windows. Tom could be seen in the video quickly rushing to the rear cellar window and unlatching it open. A smile could be seen on Drew's face as he watched the video.

He called Jack Mullen with his findings. They arranged to visit Tom Holt at his home in East Providence that night.

"I'm Tom Holt. What can I do for you?" he asked.

"I'm Detective Jack Mullen from the Attleboro Police Department, and this is Drew Diamond, an investigator with the Assurance Insurance Company. Do you work for the Superior Oil Company in Attleboro?" the detective asked.

"Yes, I'm a serviceman for them."

"Were you at 47 Melody Road in Cumberland today to service a furnace?" Mullen asked.

"Yes, of course. I repaired a furnace there this morning. Is there a problem?"

Drew pulled out his laptop and opened the cover. He punched in a few keys, and handed the laptop to Mullen.

"Is this you in the basement of that home this morning, Mr. Holt?"

"Yes, it is," he answered.

"Are you always in the habit of unlocking cellar windows in the homes you service?" Mullen asked as he watched Holt's reaction to the video in front of him.

"Oh, that, no, it was rather warm in the basement this morning, and I opened the window to get some air."

"And you left the property without closing the window?" Mullen asked.

"Oh my, I guess I did. Did something happen in the basement? It didn't rain through the window, did it?"

"So, you didn't leave the window unlocked deliberately?"

"Why would I do that? What is this about?"

"Mr. Holt, do you unlatch cellar windows at other houses you service?"

"On occasion, I might have."

"And have you always done so when the owner was not in the basement with you?"

"I can't really remember that. What's this all about, please?"

"It's about homes being burglarized because the intruder came through an unlatched cellar window, that's what this is about. And several of the homes you serviced have been burglarized in the last month. Quite a coincidence, wouldn't you say? And when I look at this video, I don't see the window open at all, just unlocked. So much for getting fresh air, wouldn't you say?"

"I'm not a burglar, and I resent what you're implying. I'm six feet tall and I weigh over two hundred pounds. Do I look like I could fit through a cellar window? Are we done here? Unless I'm being accused of committing a crime, I think you should leave my house, now."

"Maybe you can't fit through that window, or any of the other cellar windows, Mr. Holt, but you certainly could have an accomplice who does fit? Let's hope none of your next service calls are burglarized. I don't think that would be a coincidence, would it?

"We're done here. Leave my house, or arrest me, Detective. But we're done talking right now. Please leave."

As the two left Holt's home, Mullen smiled as he looked at Diamond.

"We'll be assigning a few officers outside his home for a few days. And we'll have at least one of our unmarked cars following him around wherever he goes, and whoever he meets. If he's working with a woman, we'll find her."

"Just another quick observation, Jack, but the cellar window he unlatched was not the nearest window to where he was working. Why would he unlatch a window in the back of the house when there was one right behind him?" Drew told Mullen.

"Damn it, Drew, you must have been a heck of a detective in Worcester. I never thought of that. So, he's our guy, but we need to see who he's hooked up with."

After the two men left his house, Tom Holt was quite nervous, breaking into a cold sweat. In his mind, the small amount he received for simply leaving a cellar window unlocked was no big deal. Heck, he never even met the person he gave the information to, but gladly welcomed the two hundred dollars per name, anonymously placed in an envelope in his mailbox. *Should I call the number to let you know the police are getting close?* he pondered. *Or should I just stop calling the number and not open any more windows?* He opted for the latter. He no longer would open any cellar windows. Whoever the contact was would have to be on his own from now on.

At eight o'clock that night, two detectives sat in the dark in their unmarked car about one hundred yards from Holt's home. Holt had not left his house that night. Stakeouts are probably the most boring assignment a detective can have. The detective could literally sit in his car all night long, and nothing would happen. One of the hardest chores was to stay awake during the night hours.

At nearly eleven that night, an SUV drove past the detectives' car and proceeded toward the front of Tom Holt's house. The car stopped briefly, right in front of his mailbox as the tail lights went on. A hand stuck out of the SUV, opened the mailbox, and inserted something before closing the box. Immediately, the detectives started their car and began to follow the SUV as it veered out of sight on an adjacent street.

Suddenly, the SUV turned off its headlights and travelled from street to street in complete darkness. There were few street lights on this rural road. Quickly, the SUV pulled into a driveway and shut the engine. The driver bent down, out of sight, as the detectives' vehicle drove by. A minute later, the SUV backed out of the driveway and headed in the opposite direction, still with its headlights off. A mile later, the headlights were turned on and the car disappeared into the night. Sydney had just had her closest call, and she was terrified at the thought that she could actually be caught. A sudden realization swept over her, and she was shaking all the way home. She pulled into her apartment complex, went straight up to her unit, and as she entered her apartment, locked the door behind her and began to weep.

She hung her car keys on the hook next to the door, and as she entered the kitchen, she spotted the blinking light on her answering machine. She hit the replay button and listened to the message.

"Hi, Sydney, this is Drew. I know the closing on the condo isn't for another week or so, but I was just calling in to say hello, and to see if you were free for lunch or dinner in the next couple of days. If you're interested, give me a call at 762-3700, extension 212, or on my cell phone, 401-368-3200. Have a nice night."

The message seemed to calm her. Suddenly, her fears were overridden with a smile at the message she had just listened to. With that thought in mind, she jumped into the shower and let the warm water add to calm her even further, as she lathered up with soap and began to slowly rinse off the suds covering the small tattoo on her neck, to the bottom of her feet.

The thought of suddenly having a man pay her much attention was a feeling she had long ago abandoned when the doorbell had rung ten years earlier and two uniformed soldiers stood at her door. She admitted to herself that there was a maturity to Drew Diamond that she liked, and anyone paying this much attention to her deserved at least the courtesy of a return phone call.

She would call Drew in the morning.

CHAPTER 11

PORTLAND TO NEW YORK

Bruno Gambardella was not happy to learn that Richie Volpe had disappeared, and that Richie's mother had not reported for work at the diner for nearly a week. Some guy had shown a receipt for all the furnishings in their apartment, and there was no trace of where they had driven off to.

At first, Bruno wired a photo of Richie to a private detective in the Hilton Head, South Carolina area, hoping that he had gone there as he had mentioned. In Bruno's mind, he really had no idea how much Richie knew about the family business. He didn't care. It was a loose end, and Bruno did not like unfinished business. It was not the family way of correcting a potential leak in the organization.

Garrett Hunter's cell phone buzzed, and he pressed the message icon on the phone. The text message said, "Ready to deliver packages to NYC. Text me for location of our meeting. Hope you are well. Waldo." Garrett began typing a reply on his phone. "7pm, Thursday, Expo Center, S.E. Expressway, N.E. Jewelers Show. Garrett."

Finally, Garrett thought. I can get back a sizable amount for the pearls when they are sold in New York. While Richie was going to the Big Apple, he would give him the recent jewelry Sydney was about to drop off the next morning. He preferred not to resell the jewelry in the same state as he bought it in. He remembered the blunder of his youth when he tried to resell stolen cars and spent five years in prison for doing so. If a piece of jewelry had some identifying mark on it, and he somehow missed seeing it, the former owner might accidentally stumble onto it in his store, and he would have some explaining to do. Garrett was cautious, and never wanted to be under suspicion of wrongdoing by the police. Being identified as a jewelry store used to fence items was not good for his relationship with the local police.

The jewelry expo show on Thursday consisted of over a hundred tables of jewelry. Hunter Jewelry would be displaying its products at the show for the fifth year in a row.

Brynn McDaniel, the owner of a jewelry wholesale house in New York, would be there, not as a vendor, but to visit each jeweler at his booth to drum up his business with the retail stores in New England. Ironically, some of McDaniel's items were purchased from individuals hoping to unload family personal items at reasonable prices.

Unlike the infamous "We Buy Gold and Jewelry" ads for purchases made in hotel rooms at ridiculously low prices, a New York wholesaler's reputation was far better. Garrett had dealt with Brynn before, even with some items Richie had fenced through Hunter Jewelry.

The show went from ten in the morning to nine at night. Security was very tight, as some jewelers had over a million dollars of gems displayed at their booths. McDaniel would take a look at Garrett's items for sale, and offer him a flat sum for the entire lot, normally around thirty to forty percent of their retail value. But the transaction would not take place at the show, since he was not an authorized vendor. Vendors seeking to buy or sell items to or from Brynn would set up appointments with him in New York.

As Brynn analyzed the pearl necklace and matching ring, he looked up at Garrett in amazement.

"Garrett, this is the mother lode of pearls. I don't see this very often. This should do quite well to one of my customers in the high end market. Do you know what they sell for?" McDaniel asked.

"They're insured for $100,000."

"Shall we say $35,000 for the lot?"

"I was thinking more like $40,000. There's about $10,000 in all the other stuff besides the pearls."

"I can go to $37,000, but that's it," McDaniel answered.

"Here's the combination to my suitcase. I'll be using another man to take them to your office. He'll go by Waldo, and will have all the items with him."

"How soon can he be in New York?"

"He can be there on Monday morning. Name the time."

"Eight in the morning. I'll be watching for him. As always, it's a pleasure doing business with you."

He left Garrett's booth at noon and proceeded to visit the next booth and the one after that, covering all the booths at the show before he left. His goal was to be back to Logan Airport in Boston by six o'clock, in time to catch the seven o'clock shuttle to LaGuardia.

At six-thirty at night, Richie appeared. He was letting his facial hair grow, wore black horn-rimmed glasses, and was wearing a tie and jacket under a topcoat. Garrett was pleasantly surprised by the change in appearance, and shook his hand as he stood facing him in front of the booth.

"You're early, I like that. Everything went well with Gambardella, I take it. You look great."

"He said he was okay with me leaving, but a half hour later at my apartment, he sent two guys there. Luckily, I got out of there before they saw me. I picked up my mom, and we were gone."

"I don't want to know where you are. That way, I can't tell anyone if I don't know."

Garrett reached into a trunk under the counter and pulled out a large satchel. Inside the satchel was a velour bag containing the jewelry items he had just shown Mc-Daniel, and a briefcase with a combination lock on it.

"You will go to 237 Fifth Avenue in New York early on Monday morning. You must be there by eight sharp.

Brynn McDaniel is the guy who will be expecting you. He will analyze the items in the bag, and then ask you for the briefcase. He has the combination. He will put the money we agreed on in the briefcase and lock it. You will drive back to New England once the transaction has been completed. At six at night, I will meet you at the 110 Grill in Hopkinton, Massachusetts. I'll be at the bar. We'll have a drink and a bite to eat, and I'll have some more money for you over the two thousand I gave you last week. What's your favorite drink?" Garrett asked.

Richie wrote all the information down. Garrett could tell he was nervous. This was likely his biggest job yet, and he knew that Garrett had gone out on a limb for him. He didn't want to disappoint him.

"Jack Daniel's and Coke," he answered.

Richie repeated his instructions from Garrett, just to be sure he had everything right.

"Relax. When you leave the show, make sure no one is following you. I'm guessing you and your mom are some-where up north. Once you're certain you don't have any-one following you, you're golden. On Monday morning, be sure to leave early enough for New York to be there before eight o'clock. I don't care if you fly, drive, or ride the bus or the train to the city, so long as you get there on time. Brynn is a very busy man, and if you're late, he may not have time to see you. Like you were tonight, better to be early," Garrett emphasized.

"Thanks, Garrett. I won't forget this."

"I'll have your drink on the bar for you on Monday night. See you then."

Richie was very cautious as he drove up Route 95 toward New Hampshire and Maine. When he stopped for gas at eight o'clock, he called his mother to see if she was okay, and whether she had eaten dinner yet.

"Hi, Richie. I finished the leftover macaroni we had on Tuesday. Are you all right?" she asked.

"I'm fine, Mom. I should be home around nine or so. I have some good news to tell you when I get there," he answered. He then turned off his smartphone and headed for Portland. He arrived an hour later.

"I got a job delivering and picking up jewelry for a big jeweler. I'll have to go to New York every so often, because that's where all the stuff comes from. But it'll give me some time to look for something around here. I'm still thinking about doing real estate, and I might take a course at one of the colleges nearby to get myself ready for any real estate test I need to take to get licensed. After that, I'll try to hook up with an agency in Portland."

"I want to help. I can't just sit around the house all day long. For nearly twenty five years, I've held two jobs. If I have to stay home all day, I'll go crazy," she said.

"First things first, Mom. Let's get your knees looked at by a specialist up here, and hear what he has to say. If knee replacements are the way to go, we can talk about you going back to work after that."

"Okay, that would be nice. But that's going to take a lot of money or some good health insurance coverage."

"I'm working on it. Just give me some time."

At midnight the following Monday morning, Richie began the drive to New Haven, Connecticut, a five-hour drive. To save money, he believed it was the cheapest way to get there. Hopefully, he would not run into much traffic at this early hour. He would leave his car at the New Haven train station, and take the commuter train into New York's Penn Station, arriving at seven o'clock. From there, the walk to 237 Fifth Avenue would take only five to ten minutes.

Everything went on schedule, and he entered Brynn McDaniel's office at seven-thirty five. The secretary relayed his arrival to Brynn, and he opened his office door a few minutes later.

"You must be Waldo, Garrett's courier. Come on in. I like a man who is early," he said as he extended his hand to Richie.

"Nice to meet you, Mr. McDaniel. Mr. Hunter told me to be prompt, because he said you were a busy man."

"Well, Garrett is right. Let's take a look at the merchandise you're bringing in," he answered as he closed his office door.

Richie pulled out the velvet pouch, and handed it to McDaniel. The review process took about ten minutes. He then referred to his notes, and was satisfied that the goods were in order as promised.

"Do you have the briefcase, Waldo?" he asked.

Richie pulled the briefcase from the satchel and handed it to McDaniel, who rose and went into a separate room.

"I'll be right back."

Within five minutes, McDaniel returned, and handed the briefcase to Richie.

"I believe we are done, Waldo. Give my best to Garrett, and I hope to see you again on your next trip to New York."

Richie placed the briefcase in his satchel, zipped it closed, and slung it over his shoulder, clasping the strap with a firm grip. He knew what was in the briefcase, and was not about to let it out of his sight or his grip. He walked back to Penn Station at twenty minutes after eight, and was on a train back to New Haven by nine, expecting to arrive there by eleven o'clock. The drive from New Haven to Hopkinton, Massachusetts would take only about two hours, so he decided to stop for lunch at a highway courtesy station along the way. That still would get him to Hopkinton around two o'clock, way too early. Garrett would not be there until six, four hours later.

It was early February, and the temperatures in New England hovered in the teens, with an occasional warming trend into the thirties. As he pulled up to a gas station in Hopkinton, he asked the attendant inside the attached convenience store where the local library was. Once there, he asked the librarian at the reference desk if the library carried any books on becoming a real estate agent. She told him to grab a seat in the reference room lounge, and in a short while brought him several pieces to read on the subject. All the while, he carried the satchel with the briefcase inside, never so much as releasing his grip for a second. The next several hours were very productive as Richie read countless articles on the subject of real estate agents. Before he realized it, it was five-thirty, and the library would be closing at six.

As he left the library, he thanked the librarian for her help, jumped into his car, and drove the short distance to the 110 Grill.

He walked into the restaurant five minutes later and was surprised to see Garrett already sitting at the bar.

"Wow, I'm impressed, Richie. Right on time. Everything went well in New York?" Garrett asked.

"As far as I can tell, everything went smoothly. Mr. McDaniel doesn't waste any time. I was there before eight, and out the door by eight-thirty. Here's the satchel with the briefcase inside."

"I believe you have a Jack Daniel's and Coke sitting right there in front of you. I'll be right back," he responded.

Garrett walked to the parking lot in semi-darkness, and beeped his car keys to unlock the front door of his car. He drove a four-door 2017 Cadillac Escalade with tinted windows everywhere. After he entered the driver's side of the vehicle, he shut the door and locked the car. He removed the briefcase from the satchel, and entered the combination numbers on the locked case.

The money inside the case was meticulously piled in neat rows. Sitting on top of the money was a note from McDaniel indicating the case was locked before he returned it to Waldo. Garrett quickly counted the cash...$37,000. McDaniel had included the additional two thousand to reflect the rubies and sapphires the blonde had brought in the previous Monday morning.

He counted out four thousand dollars, and placed it in a large envelope. He inserted the envelope in the inside pocket of his suit coat, relocked the briefcase, and slipped it under the passenger seat of the car. As he beeped the door to the lock position, he physically tried each door to be sure they were all locked.

"How's the drink? Here's to a long and prosperous relationship, or until you are settled in a new occupation," he said as he toasted his new accomplice.

They continued small talk on how easy the whole transaction occurred, until they decided to order dinner. Before dinner arrived, Garrett reached into his coat pocket and handed Richie the envelope.

"There's $4,000 in the envelope, and you can forget about the first $2,000 I gave you a week ago. We are square."

"I can't take this kind of money. It's too much."

"It's not too much for me, and your time and expenses to and from New York are clearly worth it to me. I don't know when the next trip will happen, but it might take a while. I'll keep in touch by texting you on your smartphone. That worked well this time around."

By eight, they parted ways and Richie entered Route 495 North. He would be home by ten.

He breathed a sigh of relief as he entered his new apartment in Portland. His mother's smile was all he needed to see.

CHAPTER 12

FIRST DATE

Although Sydney slept reasonably well on Tuesday night, the thought of actually getting caught in someone else's home scared the living hell out of her as she rose for breakfast early Wednesday morning. February real estate transactions were slow, except for apartments or condos. It's hard to visualize the full appearance of the landscape when there is snow on the ground. Add to that the thought of moving in during winter months, and what you have is a slow real estate market.

Her commissions during this period were quite low, and it was easy to imagine the glee at getting a much needed commission for the sale of the condo to Drew. She was faced with a dilemma...how to earn enough money during the slow real estate season to keep her afloat until spring. The activity of the night before was too close a call. She realized that one or more of her accomplices had been discovered somehow. *Do I lay low for a while, or do I perform my own surveillance with the servicemen I am dealing with? Let's wait and see if I get any more calls from any of my four contacts,* she pondered.

"Hi, Drew," she pleasantly answered after he had picked up the ringing phone in his office at nine o'clock in the morning. "Where exactly is your office? It just dawned on me that I never even asked you what you do for a living."

"Well, hello to you, Sydney. By calling my direct line, I simply answer like it was a personal call. But I work for Assurance Casualty & Property Insurance as a claim investigator."

"No wonder you liked the location of the condo. It's only about ten minutes from Assurance…the one on Washington Highway, I assume?"

"That's the one. I get to use my former police experience when I'm reviewing claims by our policyholders. Are you free for lunch? Trattoria Romana is right up the street from here. Or we can do dinner there if that's too quick for you?" he asked.

"Tonight would be better. Wednesdays at the agency we usually have a luncheon meeting in the office with the manager."

"I can pick you up at six. Just give me an address, and I'll be there," he answered.

"2065 Mendon Road, Apartment 510. It's called Chimney Hill Apartments. I live alone, so the place is small, but it's okay for me right now. I'll see you then."

Drew had a smile from ear to ear. She had actually accepted his invitation. He was like a teenager getting ready for his first date. It had been a while since he had taken a woman to dinner, and Sydney was younger than most women he knew. She made him feel younger than his age. She even had told him he looked only in his forties. The afternoon seemed to crawl by, and somehow he couldn't concentrate on any of the cases he was working on. He shuffled files around, opened a few for a minute or two only, and checked his calendar, his email messages, anything to pass the time away. What should he wear? It was February, still very cold. A suit was too dressy...maybe a nice shirt with a sweater? He would surely go back to his apartment by four-thirty to change first.

He rang the doorbell at number 510. As he stood there, quite fidgety, Sydney opened the door and smiled. She looked dazzling in a pair of black slacks, wearing a white blouse, topped by a thick knit light blue sweater. Her short hair was combed perfectly, and her face had warmth written all over it. She wore little makeup or eye liner, she didn't need it. Her dark brown eyes sparkled, and her smile said it all.

"Hello, Drew, welcome to my place. Come on in while I get my coat and gloves."

As she walked toward the bedroom, Drew took the time to scan the apartment. He stood in the foyer which displayed an open concept living room, leading directly into a kitchen. The living room was quite cozy, with a sofa and recliner facing a big-screen TV. To the far side was a granite kitchen island surrounded by stainless steel appliances and ample cabinet space above the kitchen counter.

The hallway between the two rooms led to the bedroom and a full bath. Perhaps he would visit the bedroom at a later date…optimism abounded.

Sydney emerged from the bedroom in a knee-length woolen coat, buttoned nearly to the top, where a white scarf surrounded her neck and came down the front of the coat. She looked gorgeous. He smiled.

"Shall we?"

Dinner at Trattoria was wonderful. Sydney's curiosity about Drew's line of work was conversational at best. He emphasized that his role at the company was to verify the legitimacy of claims filed with the insurer. To Sydney, this seemed rather a mundane job for a former career police officer, but the curiosity peaked more when he elaborated.

"I basically handle investigating high-priced burglaries and arson cases in Rhode Island, Massachusetts, and Connecticut. There's been a string of burglaries in the area over the last few months. One woman filed a claim for some pearls stolen right out of her dresser. They were insured by us for $100,000. Can you believe a strand of pearls and a matching ring could be worth that much?"

She nearly choked on her shrimp cocktail as he mentioned the value.

"Are you kidding me? I'd be afraid to wear them anywhere. What if the necklace broke? Can you see me on my knees making sure I have every pearl? How many pearls can be on such a necklace?" she asked.

"I think there were about forty pearls."

"But how do you catch whoever did this? How do you

go about finding this guy? Does he leave clues, finger-prints, or anything like that?"

"First of all, I think it's a woman, or one really small guy who can fit through cellar windows. Sometimes there are video cameras on the property, and you catch a decent image. Sometimes a jeweler calls us because the burglar tries to fence the jewelry. If we've sent out photos of the items to jewelry stores soon enough after the break-in, we might get lucky."

"When you said you worked for an insurance compa-ny as a claims investigator, I thought you were like a guy who looks at a car wreck to see what the damages were. This sounds much more exciting," she said.

"Arson cases are much more difficult to solve. Every time a factory burns down, everyone thinks it was deliber-ate and for the insurance money, especially if the factory was vacant. That's very hard to prove, and we work closely with experts from the local fire departments. And it's not every fire department that has an expert in that area. For-tunately, I don't have too many of these each year."

"How about residences, single or multi-family hous-es. Are many of those deliberately burned down?"

"I wouldn't say many, but once in a while the fire de-partment smells gasoline in a basement of a house, some-times the house is vacant, but sometimes the house is oc-cupied. Some people are lucky they weren't there at the time of a fire."

"Oh, I'm sorry. I'm talking too much about your line of work. It makes my real estate work sound overly bor-ing."

"I think my son would disagree with you on that. He and Claire love the real estate business."

By nine, they both realized they had been at the restaurant for nearly three hours. Drew hailed the waiter and settled the bill as they prepared to leave. They arrived at Chimney Hill ten minutes later.

"Thank you for a wonderful dinner. No need for you to come up five stories. I can see myself up."

She leaned across the passenger seat, and kissed him tenderly on the lips. She gently withdrew herself from his arms, and opened the door to his car.

"Hopefully, we will do this again soon," she said as she smiled at him.

He was breathless. Before he could say a single word, she was inside the lobby of the apartment house, and out of sight. A few minutes later, as she stepped from the elevator on the fifth floor, she said to herself, *He investigates burglaries! Oh shit, the guy I'm dating is trying to find evidence to catch me. So much for my side job.*

She entered her apartment, flipped on the lights, and removed her coat and scarf. When she hung the coat in her bedroom closet, she saw the black duffle bag that contained her new spandex leggings, her black gloves, and her hat.

"It's time for me to lay low."

She kicked off her shoes, and looked at the notepad on her nightstand. "47 Melody Road, Cumberland." She turned on her laptop on the small desk in the corner of the bedroom, and typed the address on Google. Up came a photo of the two-story home, and a note that read "This house is not currently on the market." She then went to the Town of Cumberland website and clicked on "Real Estate Data" and then "Online Database." From that screen, she typed in the street address. A new screen appeared showing the current owner, Arthur and Roberta Donnelly. The name meant nothing to her, but she jotted it down next to the address on the notepad.

Next, she typed in Assurance Property and Casualty Insurance on Google, and accessed their website. Under the category of Departments, she was able to reach an area for Claims Investigation. On that page, she was able to see Drew's name as the Chief Investigation Officer. This was exactly as Drew had told her at dinner.

Here she was, at the outset of her first relationship in ten years, and she was faced with a dilemma. *How do I date a man whose job it is to find a burglar, and have him arrested for committing the crime, when I am that burglar?*

Perhaps this would all go away if she ceased robbing residences. Her second job would be temporarily put on hold. She really liked Drew Diamond.

CHAPTER 13

THE CLOSING AND THE COINCIDENCES

On Thursday morning, Drew sat at his desk, still thinking about Sydney and the night before. While it was easy to understand his sexual attraction to a beautiful thirty-two year old widow, he wondered what she saw in a fifty-six year old man.

By eleven that morning, he had dialed the Morgan Realty office number several times, hanging up each time as the phone began to ring. At eleven-thirty, his phone rang.

"Drew, this is Sydney. First, thank you again for dinner last night. It was wonderful. And I have good news. The owner of your new condo is anxious to complete the deal, so I set up a closing date for next Monday afternoon. There's a lot of paperwork involved, but without a mortgage, you've made my job a lot easier. How does two o'clock sound?"

"That's awesome. I can get a painter in there either next week or the week after, and get a carpet installer lined up too."

"Assuming everything goes well on Monday, you can move in whenever you want. Did I tell you that I also do interior decorating?"

"And I bet for a very reasonable price," he added with a chuckle. "Shall we celebrate?"

"Do you celebrate everything?" she asked with a smile that he could visualize.

"Well, not everything, but this is only my second property in over thirty years. That seems like a worthy event, wouldn't you say?"

"Okay, I'm convinced. But what if I order a pizza and you bring the wine. Six-thirty at my place. You're forcing me to work all weekend on your closing papers, if they're to be ready by Monday afternoon."

"You can kick me out whenever you're ready. You do realize we will have to celebrate again on Monday night after the closing. Tonight is really only a pre-celebration," he stated as he hung up the phone.

He arrived at her apartment at a quarter after six. She had ordered a pepperoni pizza from Dominos, which was to be delivered at six-thirty. He asked her for a corkscrew for the bottle of Duckhorn he picked up at the liquor store across from Chimney Hill Apartments, and poured some in each glass she had placed on the kitchen island.

"To Monday's closing and a real celebration that

night. And to my new interior decorator. I don't have a clue about wall colors and matching carpets," he said.

She laughed as they clanged glasses and looked at each other very amorously. He put down his wine glass, and took hers from her hands and placed it next to his on the counter. He pulled her forward toward him and kissed her warmly. She did not resist his advance. Quite the contrary, she wanted more. The two of them had been living alone for too long, and the feeling of suddenly finding a mate was welcomed by both of them. In the midst of their kisses, they both began to grope at each other, until the doorbell rang.

"Great timing," she said, "but hold that thought for now," she continued as she straightened herself up before answering the door. Drew handed her a twenty dollar bill, which she hesitated taking, but he insisted. Sydney, in turn, handed the change to Drew after giving the delivery boy the customary tip.

He took the pizza from Sydney and placed it on the counter.

"You do have a microwave, don't you?"

He kissed her again and again. The motions that followed by both of them soon led to the bedroom. The passion continued until they began to remove clothing and fall into the bed. The pizza would have to wait.

An hour later, Sydney rose first and indicated she would take a quick shower.

"I think the pizza needs to be reheated right about now. I'm not so sure the microwave is needed though. It looks to me like if you merely hold it for a few minutes, it will be quite hot," she said as she smiled his way and disappeared into the bathroom.

Drew laid in bed for a few more minutes, and casually rose and sat at the side of the bed as he rose. He noted the memo pad on the nightstand, and glanced down as he turned on the lamp.

"Arthur Donnelly, 47 Melody Lane, Cumberland"

He quickly turned the lamp off, got dressed, and walked into the kitchen very puzzled.

How does she know Art? He wondered.

He placed the pizza into the microwave and punched the timer for two minutes. While the pizza was heating, he poured two more glasses of wine, and lit the candles on her kitchen table where Sydney had arranged two place settings. He had just had the most memorable experience he could have had in over two years, yet he suddenly had questions spinning in his head when she reappeared in a terry cloth robe. He approached her, kissed her again and handed her a wine glass.

"That was wonderful. Where have you been all my life?"

She smiled and turned to sit down at the table. His face dropped.

"You have a tattoo on your neck. Let me see."

"When Bruce died, he was awarded the Purple Heart Medal posthumously. A month later, in a moment of weakness and loneliness, I had the tattoo of a purple heart placed on my neck. The guy at the tattoo parlor said a lot of women who lost a husband in combat have a Purple Heart tattoo. I forgot I even had it."

Drew wolfed down the pizza and wine, trying desperately not to show any emotion at seeing the tattoo, the same tattoo he had zoomed in on from the Simonton Jewelry video. *How many people really have a tattoo of a purple heart on their neck?*

Sydney kissed him goodnight, and Drew reluctantly left her apartment at nine. He had so many questions, but now was not the time.

* * *

Meanwhile, Richie had scrutinized the want ads for jobs in the Portland area. The University of Southern Maine Athletic Department was seeking a maintenance worker for full-time work year-round. There were thirteen athletic facilities on campus, all of them requiring upkeep. In the spring months, the maintenance crew would focus on resurfacing the gym floors, repainting the locker facilities, daily cleaning of all the classrooms and coaches' offices. In late spring, there was mowing of all the baseball and athletic fields, and grounds preparation before athletic contests, including track and field events. Richie thought this to be a beginning. There would be plenty of fresh air and sunshine, and he didn't mind the physical aspect of the job. The hours were seven to three, and there was opportunity for overtime hours during and after athletic nighttime events. The pay was $17.50 per hour, plus medical and retirement benefits. He could add his dependent mother on his medical coverage, and he could take courses at the college at no cost.

He was nervous on the day of the interview, as he sat

down in front of the human resources recruiter at the school.

"Why do you believe we should give you this job, Mr. Lamb? What qualifications do you bring to this position? I didn't notice you mentioning any past experience in the maintenance area on your application form," the recruiter asked.

"I don't have any experience in maintenance, sir. As a matter of fact, I basically did pickup and delivery in my last job, but the work wasn't steady enough, and I couldn't support my mother with erratic paychecks. She has bad knees and can hardly walk. I need a full-time job to do that, sir, and I'm strong physically, and can do a lot of work in one day. I just need a chance to prove myself. You wouldn't be disappointed, I can promise you that," he said with sincerity.

"How do we know you're not just going to take this job until something better comes along?"

"You don't know. But then again, that goes for anybody working on this campus, sir, even you. If someone gave you an offer for a lot more money, doing the same thing you're doing right now, but at another school, you'd at least think about it. In my case though, without a lot of education, the chances are slimmer that this would happen. I can only tell you that for as long as I work here, I will be loyal to this school. Hopefully, that will be for a long time."

The recruiter pondered Richie's response for a minute, and liked his frankness. Internally, he agreed with his assessment of the job. He offered the job to him for a three-month probation, at which time, if everything was satisfactory, the job would become permanent. Richie would begin the following Monday.

Rona was pleased for her son, and even happier to hear about the medical coverage. Perhaps soon, her knees could be repaired. Richie was not aware how much pain his mother suffered from her knees. She never made a fuss, and one day soon, there hopefully would be nothing to fuss about anyway.

CHAPTER 14

SYDNEY FLETCHER

Drew was up late on Friday night. Was it the passion and the romantic setting he and Sydney had earlier, or was it the sudden thought that she could be his mysterious female burglar? He had to find out before this relationship got any more serious than the direction it was headed in. He felt alive again after a hiatus of over two years of wandering around aimlessly. Each of his two children was in a meaningful relationship. That meant they were spending a great deal of time with their significant other, and less time with him, as it should be. Sydney made him want to become active, not merely sexually, but she made him feel like he could do things a thirty-year old could do, not an easy task for someone who had incurred open heart surgery in his early fifties.

But, who really was this woman? Where did she come from? He needed to know more, and yet, he feared for what he would learn, given the similarities with a woman he was chasing for multiple crimes.

"Sydney, I know this might sound strange, but I'd really like to get to know you more," he began to say on a Sunday morning phone call.

"I own a cabin in northern New Hampshire that I seldom go to. It's quite cozy, but pretty isolated from civilization. It's got electricity from a generator, and a heating and cooking stove that's in working order. I was wondering if you'd be interested in spending a few days up there with me after the closing on Monday. I'm not sure if you're a woodsy kind of person or not?" he asked.

With thoughts of the activities of Friday evening still very much on her mind, Sydney was not about to say no.

"You're actually asking me to spend time in the state I was born in. How can I refuse? I'll ask my boss for the rest of the week off. Do you want to leave on Tuesday or Wednesday? Where exactly is this place of yours anyway?" she asked.

"In the woods of Pittsburg, New Hampshire. There's only one road that goes through it, and then you're in Canada. Have you ever snowmobiled?"

"I was born in Clarksville, just south of Pittsburg. There are more moose in that area than people. How in the world did you ever get a cabin in the snowmobile capital of New England? And yes, I do snowmobile. The trails up there go all the way into Canada or to Maine and Vermont. Sounds like we like the same things."

"Great, I've got the snowmobile suits and the machines up there, and we can stop at the local grocery store to pick up supplies. Let's shoot for Tuesday at eight. I'm sure we'll have some stories to share."

On Monday morning, Drew asked his associate to put a list of tattoo artists together. He told the associate to find out if, indeed, many women had a tattoo of a purple heart on their neck, as Sydney had mentioned. Perhaps the tattoo was more common than he was aware of. As an experienced investigator, he did not want to jump to a conclusion that Sydney's tattoo automatically pegged her as the burglar he was after. He asked the associate to text him with whatever information he would find. What did trouble him though, was that the tattoo was coupled with a recent dog bite on her right leg, the same leg the dog bit in the recent video of the burglar fleeing the house with the dog. One coincidence he could handle. Two coincidences were troubling.

The closing on the condo on Monday afternoon went smoothly, and Drew and Sydney decided on an early dinner celebration at Siena Restaurant, nearly walking distance from the Smithfield office of Morgan Realty. After dinner, he dropped her off at that office, and she drove home. Drew would pick her up at eight o'clock on Tuesday morning for their trip to Pittsburg. He had already made arrangements with the maintenance service to be sure the cabin was in perfect condition by Tuesday afternoon, that it wasn't rented for the rest of the week, and that there was plenty of firewood near the wood burning stove and fireplace. He also told them to be sure the generator was filled with gasoline, and that several extra gas cans were filled as well.

On Tuesday morning, they left for Pittsburg, a six hour drive and over two hundred fifty miles away. They planned to make two stops, one at ten for coffee and a stretch break, and the second for lunch at one o'clock. They expected to reach the cabin at three in the afternoon after a brief stop at the general store. Everything went as planned.

Sydney was pleasantly surprised as they approached the cabin. The exterior, in a log cabin style, was in excellent condition. As they entered the front door, they were greeted by a warm cabin, as the wood burning pot belly stove was blazing. Wood had also been carefully placed in the fireplace with kindling, awaiting Drew to light it whenever he chose. On the kitchen table was an unopened bottle of red wine, two wine glasses, a filled ice bucket, and a covered tray of cookies.

"Very impressive, Mr. Diamond," she said with a smile. "This is not just a cabin in the woods. It's more like a chalet," she added.

After she helped him bring in the supplies and their suitcases from the car, she took off her coat and began a self-tour of the cabin. Drew himself was pleased to see all the improvements his son had made in the last few years. Wall to wall carpeting in the bedroom, fully insulated walls covered by finished pine boards, including a wood-paneled A-frame ceiling, all indeed looked like a room in a chalet. The bathroom was now tiled, and a vanity had been installed near the toilet. There was a tub installed as well, but hot water would have to come from a kettle on the stove, if a bath was intended. The living room, aside from having a stone fireplace, had a wide-screen television.

"How do you get any TV stations way out here in the woods?" she asked.

"Take a look outside on the bedroom side of the cabin. There's a fifty foot tower that exceeds the tree line, and with the generator going, we can get about six or seven stations, a couple of them from Canada. When the weather is too bad out to ski or snowmobile, it comes in handy. I've even got a DVD player if we bring up a movie or two."

He handed her the note from the maintenance company, and she was surprised when she read it.

"Drew, my wife figured you'd be tired from the drive from Rhode Island, so she made a macaroni casserole with no meat in it, just in case you or your guest are in a vegetarian mood. It's in the oven, and should be ready by six. Just check it occasionally from five on. The oven on your oil-fired stove may just not be as accurate as we think. Enjoy, Ralph Jones. 379-6362"

"You live a charmed life, mister insurance investigator."

"This place belonged to my wife's parents. They had owned it for many years. When my wife died, I inherited it. She didn't really like to come up here. She was not an outdoor person."

"Well, my maiden name was Sydney Fletcher. I was born in Clarksville in 1987, and in 2000 I left the town for the first time after my father died in a hunting accident in Maine. He was accidentally shot by another hunter when he jumped out of a tree, and the other hunter shot where the noise came from. The hunter's name was Ralph Jones. Does the name on the note look familiar?"

"Are you serious? I've never met the man. My son is the one who usually gets messages from him about the cabin. Are you sure this is the same person?"

"Between Pittsburg and Clarksville, there are probably no more than a thousand people. How many Ralph Jones do you think there are up here? He'd be in his mid to late fifties by now. I remember him as a short balding guy who looked like George Costanza from the *Seinfeld* show. He swore he would never hold a gun again, even if his life depended on it. My mother never was the same after the accident. We moved to Rhode Island a year later in 2001. I was fourteen at the time, and graduated from LaSalle Academy in Providence in 2004. I never went to college, we couldn't afford it. After a few secretarial jobs in Providence, I joined Morgan Realty in Smithfield. I met Bruce Malone while at LaSalle. We were the same age, and he joined the Army in 2007 at age twenty. In 2008, he was deployed to Afghanistan, and was killed in 2009. When we got married in 2008, after his boot camp training, I moved with him to Fort Benning, Georgia."

"I'm glad you decided to come up here for a few days. But I had no idea that you came from up here. There's probably not too much I can tell you about the area, is there?"

"Probably not, but I wanted to come too, if only to get to know who Drew Diamond really is."

"Well, I was born in Worcester, and had my entire education there, graduating from St. John's High School in 1981. I never served in the military, and worked as a carpenter for a couple of years until joining the Worcester Police in 1983. I stayed there until my retirement in 2016, over thirty years. You met my son, Drew Junior, and I also have a daughter, Alicia, who lives in Connecticut. Both of them have fiancés. When my wife died in 2017, I needed something to help keep me occupied, and the insurance opening was mentioned to me by my son who knew people working there. The rest you know."

"When Bruce died, the Army gave me a check for $100,000, but I had so many bills to pay to cover my mom's nursing home and medical costs after she had a stroke. The money's all gone. She died of a heart attack last year. So, if I don't sell real estate, I don't make very much money. Morgan Realty has been good to me, but they have quotas to reach at every location, and will continue to carry only the agents who produce. Someday I would like to own my own agency and make money off what other agents sell."

"Claire inherited her agency when her parents died in an awful plane crash. She worked hard to make the agency a continued success. I don't see any reason why you couldn't make it on your own either," he answered.

"My son gave me the names of two eating places in Pittsburg that are worth it. One is Murphy's Steakhouse, and the other is Rainbow Grille & Tavern. Have you ever heard of either of these?" he asked. "But since Ralph Jones' wife has a casserole in the oven, we can hit one of them tomorrow night," he said.

"I'm not familiar with Murphy's, but the Rainbow Grille has been there over twenty years. It's part of the Tall Timber Lodge on Beach Road, a nice spot on Back Lake. It's a nice restaurant. And people actually go there by snowmobile at this time of year."

"Great, we can go snowmobiling in the afternoon, and plan to stop there for dinner. I think it will be okay if I don't wear a suit and tie under my snowmobile outfit," he said with a grin on his face.

"They have a change room with a shower right next to the restaurant for people coming in that way. Heck, I think they even get people from Canada who snowmobile back to Canada on trails after dinner," Sydney stated.

Drew kept checking the casserole in the oven, and sure enough, at six o'clock it was ready to serve. He lit the candles that were on the small table, while Sydney looked on with a glass of wine in her hand. She liked being pampered, but it had been quite a while since a man paid that much attention to her. Dinner was lovely, and the two continued their conversation about each other's present and past life. By seven, the dishes had been washed in the sink, using hot water from the kettle on the stove.

"I'm going out back for a minute to crank up the generator. We can use the electric lights until we go to bed. I'll see if there is anything on TV, and light up the fireplace for a while. If you want to change into a robe and use the bathroom, I should have everything going by seven-thirty. You can pour some of that hot water in the kettle in the vanity in the bathroom if you want to freshen up."

Before he went outside to start the generator, Drew

noticed the gas lights begin to flicker, and he realized the propane gas tank behind the cabin was likely running low.

"I'll turn off the gas lights once the electricity is on. I'll call Ralph, and have him bring a replacement tank tomorrow, even if we're not here."

Sydney removed her sweater as the cabin was now quite warm from the heat of the potbelly stove, along with the heat still emanating from the oven of the oil-fired stove the casserole had been in. She then kicked off her fleece-lined boots and strode around the living room carpet in her stocking feet.

Drew started the generator, and waited a few minutes before turning on the electric light switch on the outside wall of the cabin. He then turned off the propane gener-ated lamps. When he re-entered the cabin, Sydney had already lit the paper under the kindling in the fireplace. He poured two glasses of Grand Marnier over ice, and brought them to the coffee table in front of the sofa fac-ing the TV. Sydney touched Drew's cheek gently, and said she would be back shortly.

"I'll just freshen up a little, and slip on something more comfortable. I shouldn't be long."

Drew reached for his cell phone to see if he had any messages as Sydney left the room. There was one message.

Checked twenty tattoo parlors in Rhode Island and Massa-chusetts. All of them do Purple Heart tattoos for military wives who have spouses deployed overseas. Some on the neck, others on one side of a hip. ...Art.

The news brought a smile to Drew's face as he sipped his after-dinner drink. The coincidence of a tattoo and a dog bite on Sydney, he believed, was just that, a coincidence.

When Sydney reappeared ten minutes later, she was wearing a long blue fleece robe, closed from top to bottom, and tied by a matching sash. Drew had turned on the TV set. There were two college basketball games on, one of them in French, an old episode of *Seinfeld* on Channel 6, and a Montreal station carrying the Canadiens hockey team. Sydney found it remarkable that his TV had such good reception deep in the woods of Pittsburg, but expressed her ambivalence to any of the programs on. Drew slid open the drawer on the coffee table, and pulled out two DVDs, *Gladiator* and *Australia*.

"Both of these are good movies, not exactly romances, but good. *Australia* is not as gruesome, and there are a few good scenes between Nicole Kidman and Hugh Jackman. Let's try that one," she said as she picked up her glass and clanged it against his.

Drew removed his sweater and boots as he stoked the roaring fire from the fireplace. He inserted the disc into the DVD player, and the movie appeared on the screen.

"Wow, it sure is warm in here. When the fire dies down though, I'll need to stack the potbellied stove for the night. It might not last all night long, and it will get cold by early tomorrow morning."

"This robe is keeping me warm right now. It's certainly not what I have under the robe that will do the trick later on."

Drew saw this as his cue to make a move, and he did not hesitate. He approached Sydney on the sofa, and kissed her passionately. She welcomed his embrace eagerly as his hands began to move about, finally making their way to the sash on her robe. As he untied the loop and opened the robe, his hands met with the skin around her waist. He quickly tossed several pillows and cushions from the sofa to the rug in front of the fireplace, and led Sydney to the floor. She unbuttoned his shirt, and removed it as he did the same with his trousers. They were joined together for the rest of the night in front of the fireplace. A few blankets and more logs on the fire complemented the heat they both generated throughout the night.

CHAPTER 15

THE LOG CABIN AND MEMORIES

Drew awoke first on Wednesday morning, and quietly took the kettle from the stove to the bathroom where he washed and shaved. Once he was dressed, he refilled the kettle and placed it back on the stove. He gently poked at the fading embers in the fireplace, and added more kindling and a few more logs over the kindling. It was seven o'clock. He had lit two lanterns on the hearth of the fireplace. He turned the lanterns off as the sunlight beamed brightly through the kitchen window. A coffee pot was readied and placed on the stove.

He then just sat in an easy chair watching Sydney sleep, wrapped completely in two blankets with her head nestled on the throw pillows from the sofa. He had not felt this way in a very long time. This was no longer a one night affair.

Sydney woke at eight to the smell of freshly brewed coffee, which Drew was pouring in his cup at the kitchen table. She slipped on her robe, still in her stocking feet, and hugged him from behind. He put down his cup, turned, and smiled as he gave her a warm kiss and embrace. He grabbed the kettle and had her follow him into the bathroom.

"Would you like to take a warm bath before breakfast? I can warm up the tub in a minute or two, and you can soak to your heart's content."

"Oh, that would be nice. And is there a chef in the kitchen on duty?"

"Why of course. This is a five-star facility, in case you haven't noticed."

By eight-thirty, Sydney had bathed and dressed and was ready for breakfast.

"Do you like scrambled eggs and muffins?" he asked.

"Oh, that sounds great."

"Juice is in the refrigerator, and coffee is on the stove."

After breakfast, she agreed to do the dishes, while Drew prepared the two snowmobiles locked in the metal shed behind the cabin. He had earlier taken the snowsuits from the bedroom closet, and laid them out on the sofa, complete with boots, helmets, and gloves. As he started the machines and let them idle for a few minutes, Ralph Jones appeared in his pickup truck hauling a five-foot propane tank on a trailer.

"Hi, you must be Drew's father. I'm Ralph Jones. I got your text message about the propane tank being low. My fault, I should have checked it out before you got here."

"Hi, Ralph. My son Drew and I carry the same first name, so I'm Drew also. Not a problem with the propane. We cranked up the generator and used the electric lights until about eleven. With the potbelly stove and the oil-fired kitchen stove, we were fine this morning. Come on in for a moment. I'll introduce you to my guest."

They walked into the cabin as Sydney was finished cleaning up after breakfast. As she turned to greet Drew, her smile quickly turned to a frown.

"Sydney, this is Ralph Jones. Ralph, this is Sydney Malone, I think the two of you have met before."

"I'm pleased to meet you Sydney, but I don't seem to remember you. When did we meet?" Jones asked.

"You don't remember me, do you? My family and I used to live in Clarksville. My name back then was Sydney Fletcher. My father was Jim Fletcher," she answered.

Ralph Jones' extended hand was received warmly by Sydney as she stared into his eyes.

"Sydney, oh my God, it's been so long. How is your mother?"

"She died last year, Mr. Jones. I don't think she really got over dad's death. I thought the move to Rhode Island and new scenery would help, but the stroke and then the heart attack were just too much for her to handle."

As she had related earlier to Drew, Ralph Jones was a short balding man in his mid-fifties, and were it not for the prematurely greying hair, he did resemble George from the *Seinfeld* show. Tears welled in Jones' eyes as he reflected on his earlier years and his friend Jim Fletcher.

How he regretted the awful hunting accident that took Jim's life from a shot from his rifle. How does one forget such a tragedy? But Sydney could see the pain in his face as he suddenly was at a loss for words.

"Sydney, your father and I, we were…", the words never came out, but Sydney grabbed his hands and smiled.

"I know, Mr. Jones, I know. It wasn't your fault. It was an accident, and my father would be the first to tell you that. Please say hello to Mrs. Jones for me. Tell her that her casserole was delicious last night. I do remember her as a wonderful cook."

"If you get a chance before you go back to Rhode Island, please stop by to see her. I'll tell her you are here."

He then excused himself and left the cabin to install the replacement propane tank. Within ten minutes, he was gone.

"That was very nice what you said to him just now."

"Mr. Jones wouldn't hurt a fly. He's been carrying this guilt feeling for far too long. I told my mom years ago that if I ever saw him again, I'd tell him exactly what I just told him today. My dad would have wanted me to. I wonder what happened to their daughter. We were friends as teenagers. There aren't too many kids your age in these parts of New Hampshire that you can hang around with. Her name was Gloria, and she never did well in school all the time I knew her."

"I'll text him later today and ask him for you. He'll surely remember that the two of you were friends back then. But a far more important question has come up. Let's see how you do on a snowmobile this afternoon. Are we still on for the Rainbow Grille later today? Not too late though, I don't want to get lost at night on one of these trails."

"Not a problem, Mr. Investigator. All the trails are clearly marked, and with the headlights from the snow-mobiles, we just follow the signs to Pittsburg. The whole trip from the Rainbow to the cabin takes only about fifteen minutes."

While the remainder of the day was spent riding the many trails in the North Woods, Sydney could not stop thinking about her childhood friend, whom she had not communicated with in nearly twenty years. She even asked Drew on several occasions when they stopped to rest or to eat lunch if Ralph Jones had answered the text Drew had sent in the morning. Drew could sense the concern on Sydney's face, but could only shake his head in response.

Dinner at the Rainbow Grille was excellent. The wood-paneled restaurant exerted the expected winter warmth with its brick-faced fireplace, natural pine tables, and a menu to go along with the ambiance of the establishment. The return ride to the cabin proved to be un-eventful and, as they both entered the cabin, the day's long exposure to the winter air and sunshine had left them both exhausted. As Drew cranked up the fire in the fireplace, and increased the heat emanating from both the potbelly stove and the oil-fired stove, Sydney sat on the sofa to remove her snowsuit. Within five minutes, she was sound asleep. Drew placed a blanket across her lap, and sat in the lounger just staring her way. Within minutes, he, too, was sound asleep.

On Thursday morning, Sydney woke up first and quietly made her way to the kitchen. It was seven o'clock, and they expected to leave for another day on the trails late that morning. She prepared the coffee pot and placed it on the potbelly stove, which she had just loaded with wood, assuming that it would percolate faster than on the kitchen stove. She then filled the tub in the bathroom with tap water from the storage tank on the roof, and added the whole kettle of hot water. Because the kettle was too heavy for her to carry to the tub, she did it in several trips, using a five-gallon bucket each time. Though even that was a bit heavy, she managed to slowly make it to the bathroom without spilling a drop each time. She slipped off her robe, removed the clothing she had slept in, and plopped herself in the lukewarm water.

A few minutes later, as she stood to towel off, Drew stuck his head into the bathroom, and caught the sight of the day.

"Out, out, Diamond. This is sacred ground. I knew there should have been a lock on that door."

"Okay, okay, I'll go outside to empty my bladder. But nice view anyway," he said with a smile on his face.

An hour later, as they began to dress for another outside adventure, Drew could see the same concerned look on Sydney's face he had seen the afternoon before.

"What say we head toward Clarksville today? Maybe you can show me where you lived?"

"There's not much there, but I haven't been back since we left in 2001. I doubt if it's changed much, but if you want to see it, we can go there."

Snowmobiling on Thursday proved to be troublesome, as the weather was a mixture of wet snow and pure rain as the temperature was warmer than predicted this far north. Even though the snowmobile suits were waterproof, the trails were rather slick and slushy. There were few riders on the trails, and Sydney and Drew decided to head back to Pittsburg early in the afternoon.

Following soup and a sandwich for lunch at the cabin, Drew suggested they take a car ride to Clarksville and Sydney's old homestead.

"You're not going to be impressed at where I used to live. It was a small cottage with two bedrooms, a kitchen, and a living room. We didn't have much. My dad was an auto mechanic, and business was not good in the winter, except for snowmobile repairs. But my mother helped out by working at the local diner from seven to one during the week. I'm not even sure if the house is still there."

They drove no more than a few miles south to reach Clarksville. Sydney gave Drew directions to her old home, and within minutes, there it was. Nothing seemed to have changed. The outside of the house looked the same. As Drew glanced at Sydney when he slowed down in front of the house, he noticed a few tears on her face as she gazed at the house.

"Maybe we shouldn't have come. Maybe bringing up those memories was not such a good idea," he said.

"Oh, no, Drew, I'm really glad you convinced me to come here today. When I was young, I didn't think there was any reason for people to move away from here. I'm just now realizing how much this place meant to me," she answered as she placed her arm on his.

They stayed parked in front of the house for fifteen minutes, sometimes Sydney making comments about childhood events, and other moments spent in total silence. Finally, Sydney spoke.

"I need to make one more stop. I think you know where I mean. The Jones' house is just two streets over. I want to find out about Gloria."

She knocked on the front door very quietly, almost as if she was hoping no one would answer. She waited to see Diana Jones, and yet, she feared their face to face confrontation after so many years.

"Oh, my Lord, Sydney Fletcher," Diana Jones shouted as she opened the door and hugged her for what seemed over a minute. "Ralph told me you were up in Pittsburg, and staying in a cabin we take care of for the owner." She turned to Drew and shook his hand saying, "And you must be Mr. Diamond. Please come in."

There is something genuine about older homes still lived in by the owners after many years. The inside almost always looks the same as it did years ago. The Jones' residence even had the same furniture in the living room from when Sydney spent time there with Gloria, their only child.

As they sat down on the old sofa, more memories flashed before Sydney's eyes.

"You didn't just stop here today to see how I was, did you, Syd?" Mrs. Jones asked.

"Of course, I did. When I saw Mr. Jones at the cabin, I thought of you right away," she answered.

"It's very nice of you to say that, but then again, you always said nice things about people, even way back then. You want to know about Gloria, don't you?"

"Mrs. Jones, I haven't heard a word from her in eighteen years since my mom and I moved away in 2001. I sent a few Christmas cards, some birthday cards, and I put my return address on all of them, but not a word. So I stopped sending them after about eight years. Please, Mrs. Jones, what happened to her?"

"After the accident to your father, she felt so sad for you that she blamed herself for what happened. She could not talk to her father about it. They drifted apart, and she always blamed Ralph for taking away the only real friend she had. She said she could not face you anymore, that she would remind you of her father and what happened."

Tears flowed freely down Sydney's cheeks as she heard the news.

"When she heard you and your mom had moved away, things got worse. Gloria wasn't a good student in school, we both know that, and when she turned sixteen, she dropped out and started working as a waitress at Clark's Diner, where I still work today. Do you remember Jesse Sokoloski? His parents ran the trading post near Back Lake," she asked.

"No, I don't know that name. I do remember the trading post, but I didn't know who owned it."

"Well, before she dropped out of school, she met him at a school function. They were married when she turned eighteen and they moved to Portland. That was in 2005. He was a lumberman for Scott Paper Company back then, until they laid him off in 2008. Jobs were tough to find after that, so Jesse joined the Army late that year. After basic training as a mine specialist, he was sent to Afghanistan."

Mrs. Jones began to tear up herself as she recounted the tough life Gloria had had all these years.

"Jesse, a very sweet boy, was killed by a sniper in Bagram while he was dismantling a mine on an open street in the suburbs of the city. Gloria decided to stay in Portland, and she visits every few months. And she is even talking to Ralph again. Maybe she'll find somebody else in Portland, she doesn't do much, or go anywhere, and she lives alone."

"Do you have her address in Portland?" Sydney asked.

"I'll jot it down for you. Oh, she would be so surprised to hear from you again."

"My father's accident affected a lot of people, Mrs. Jones, especially your husband, and from what you've just told me, Gloria as well. I miss my father every day, but I don't blame Mr. Jones, and I most certainly never blamed Gloria for that. I lost my husband in Afghanistan, too, ten years ago, and I'm just now beginning to live again."

She looked at Drew as she spoke, and he held her hand as she continued.

"Here is my address in Rhode Island, and my telephone number. If you should hear from her, tell her I was asking about her, and, please, give her my address and telephone number."

CHAPTER 16

PORTLAND, MAINE

Due to Richie's early work shift at the university, he often opted to catch breakfast at the college cafeteria. Not only did the breakfast menu offer a wide selection of foods, but as a full-time employee, breakfast was free. Woodbury Campus Food Court opened at six thirty in the morning from Monday through Friday.

Attracted to a short order cook who worked in the food court, Richie went out of his way to constantly thank her for whatever he would order each morning.

"Hi, I'm Richie. I work in the maintenance area at the sports complex. Have you been here long?"

"Just about a year now. I used to be a waitress at the Annex Diner downtown, but the benefits here are much better, and I qualify to get a decent pension when I retire. I live alone, so I don't need medical coverage for anyone else, and you never know when you'll need to use it. Waitressing doesn't bring any benefits with it at all, especially just a diner."

"I agree completely. I take care of my mother right now, and she needs medical coverage for her bad knees. USM said I could add her on my coverage as a dependent. Where else would I get this coverage for someone with a pre-existing condition?"

Each day their conversation grew a little longer, and Richie sensed a connection between the two of them. He found out her name was Gloria from the cashier as he flashed his employee badge at the checkout counter.

"Gloria stays pretty much to herself. She doesn't say much, and doesn't hang around with any of the other women working here in the food court. I don't even know if she's married, or goes out with anybody," the cashier mentioned one morning.

After idle chat each morning for several weeks, Richie finally decided to see if Gloria would be interested in having coffee or a drink after work. At this point, he wasn't even sure if she was seeing someone else, or was married.

"Your name is Gloria, right? Can I ask if you're married or seeing someone right now? If it's none of my business, forget I asked," he blurted out one morning.

"Yes, my name is Gloria Sokoloski. And you are Richie, I remember you introducing yourself the first day you came in."

"Richard Lamb, but everybody calls me Richie."

"And no, I'm no longer married, and I'm not seeing anyone. I'm not really good company, so I keep to myself most of the time."

"Oh, I don't think so. I think you're wonderful company. You seem very concerned about what I have to say every morning, and I can't say that anyone else pays much attention to what I have to say, except maybe my mother. And my job is almost always by myself, so there isn't anyone around to talk to most of the day. I enjoy talking to you. Can I interest you in going out after work for a drink, or a cup of coffee? Or maybe you're free over the weekend. We could do dinner and a movie, if you like going to the movies?" he asked.

"Let me think about it. I haven't gone out with anyone for a few years, since my husband died. He was killed in Afghanistan, and he was the only person I ever dated. We both lived in a small town in northern New Hampshire growing up."

"I'm sorry to hear about your late husband. Sounds like military. Can I ask how he died?"

"He was working on clearing a landmine and a sniper shot him. There he is, trying to make the streets of Bagram safe to travel on, and somebody shoots him. What the hell is it with people with guns?" she asked in a very frustrated manner. "My own father accidentally shot and killed the father of my best friend on a hunting trip almost twenty years ago. He hasn't held a gun since then, and we've just finally been able to talk to each other."

"Living in Rhode Island most of my life, and growing up in the Federal Hill section of Providence, known for its connections with the mafia, I know what you mean. If it's any consolation, I don't own a gun, and I've never shot one either."

The following morning, as Richie was set to order breakfast, Gloria smiled.

"Yes, I get off at two o'clock today, and we can meet for coffee at the Annex Diner if you still want?" she said.

"I don't get off until three. Can we make it three fifteen? I'll throw in a piece of pie with coffee," he answered, brandishing a smile of his own from ear to ear.

"That's fine. I've got a few things to buy at the market next door, nothing that needs refrigeration, and I'll get that out of the way first. So, what'll it be this morning, Richie?"

Thus began several get-togethers at the diner over the next few weeks, until he finally asked her to dinner and a movie on a Friday night. She gave him her address and said she would be ready by six. Her apartment was in a two-family house on Ocean Drive, a one bedroom, three-room flat with a kitchen opening up to a small living room. The homeowners of the house had converted the upstairs of their cottage home, looking for extra income in their retirement years. At $700 per month, with heat, Gloria found the apartment to be ideal. There was hardly ever any noise, no pets barking downstairs, and she had a parking space on one side of their driveway for her small Toyota Corolla. She had lived there now for three years, and the owners were pleased that she was a quiet tenant.

Richie was nervous before he left home to pick her up. His mother could tell.

"Relax. Everything will go just fine. You and Gloria will have a nice time. She sounds like a nice woman who's been through a lot for her age. At least she doesn't have a child to take care of too. That's not so easy being a single mom, believe me, I know."

"Mom, we're doing just fine now. We can probably get your knees fixed later this spring, and you'll be up and around before the end of the summer. Then, if you want to get a job, you can do it without worrying about being on your feet for too long. This is only one dinner and a movie, but I do like her."

The drive to Gloria's apartment took no more than ten minutes at five forty-five on Friday afternoon. As he pulled up in front of the house, she came out the front door wearing a long blue overcoat, a wool beret, a matching scarf, and winter boots and gloves. Before he could get around to open the passenger door of his four-door Mercury Marquis, she had already opened the door and hopped in. The light shining from the street lamp reflected off her face as he re-entered the driver's side, and she looked radiant wearing the beret. She had let her hair down to her neck, a far cry from the pony tail she wore at the food court. Richie just smiled as he greeted her.

"I made reservations at DiMillo's On The Water for six fifteen. After that, we have two choices for movies, *Apollo 11* at the Cinemagic at eight, or *Loving Vincent* at the Patriot Cinemas at eight-thirty, your choice."

"Oh, my, I've always wanted to eat there. I've walked by it so many times."

"We can decide which movie while we eat."

Although she had not dated even once since her husband's death in 2009, nearly ten years, it was Richie who was the awkward one at dinner. He kept tugging at his sweater, believing that every wrinkle would be noticed, and he was very unsure of himself. Gloria could sense his uneasiness and tried to lighten the conversation at every opportunity she could.

"Richie, let's just have a nice dinner, talk to each other when we want to, and stay silent when we have nothing to say. You don't look like a guy who's gone out with a lot of women, and I know I haven't been to dinner with a man since my husband died. So, we have that in common. And you at least have your mom to talk to when you're at home. I talk to four walls, so I always get my way, because the walls never talk back. I haven't lost an argument in ten years."

That brought a huge smile on Richie's face, and the night suddenly just flew by as Gloria had made him so much more comfortable. In the candlelight at their table, she looked absolutely beautiful. Her long brown hair, the gray turtleneck sweater, her smooth complexion, all somehow was often hidden by a required hair net behind the counter, and an oftentimes soiled apron at work. She was five feet seven inches, and compared to Richie at six feet, they were not that far apart in height. Richie was a rock solid two hundred pounder, but his mannerisms were that of a kind and gentle person. The days of trying to look like a bully or a tough guy were behind him, and he liked being himself for a change.

They opted for the space movie and headed back to her apartment around ten at night. As he escorted her to the door of the house, he merely said goodbye to her.

"Thank you for coming out with me tonight. I really enjoyed it, and was glad I got a chance to know you better," he said as he shook her hand, almost being too formal. "Maybe we can do this again," he added.

"I would like that. I'm a bit rusty with my social habits, but I promise to do better next time, if you want a next time," she answered.

"We can talk about it on Monday morning at school. Maybe we can do just a nice dinner next weekend."

She took off her right hand glove and gently touched his face. Although Richie was not overly handsome, he did have a charm about him that Gloria liked. He placed his left hand over hers and kissed the hand warmly. A moment later, she had disappeared into the house.

* * *

In the meantime, the bitter cold and snowy weather in March made Bruno Gambardella often cranky in his behavior in Providence. Collections were down as several of his protection clients had closed shop, and following the football season, the bookmaking business would remain slow until the college basketball March Madness betting began.

He thought about Richie, and the fact that he had suddenly disappeared without a trace, and that bothered him. Richie was now considered an unnecessary risk, and Gambardella needed to rid himself of this worry. He would soon become Santucci's replacement, and Richie was a loose end.

He realized that Richie had lied to him about moving

to the Carolinas or Florida, as none of his many contacts or associates had heard a single word of his whereabouts. Investigators had no leads either. So, Gambardella decided one day in early March to visit the home of Richie's friend who had bought all the furnishings from Richie's apartment in Providence for use at their summer residence in New Hampshire. He and one of his henchmen rang the doorbell at Claude Trout's home on Thayer Street in Providence on a Saturday afternoon.

"Hello, Mr. Trout? My name is Bruno Gambardella, and I was Richie Volpe's boss before he left town with his mother a few months ago. He had mentioned he was moving to Hilton Head in South Carolina, but I haven't been able to reach him. Would you by any chance know his address? I still owe him some money, but I don't know where to send it. May we come in for a moment?" he stated as he pushed Trout backwards into the house. Trout's wife, Janice, appeared from the kitchen, hearing the commotion, and walked into the living room.

"Is everything alright in here?" she asked.

"Everything is fine, dear. You can go back into the kitchen and keep doing what you were doing," he answered.

"Oh, no, please Mrs. Trout, please join us for just a moment," Gambardella interjected. "My associate and I were asking about finding Richie Volpe. And your husband hasn't really had a chance yet to tell us."

"I have no address for Richie. All I know is that, at our bowling league one night, he asked if I was interested in several rooms of furniture for our place in Portsmouth, New Hampshire. My wife and I only bought the place about two years ago, and it was virtually empty when we bought it. So, when he said I could buy it all for $1,000, I jumped at the chance after I saw what he was selling. I've got the receipt for the stuff, but there's no forwarding address on the receipt. I do remember him talking about Hilton Head though," Trout answered.

"So you brought all this stuff to your summer home in Portsmouth? And if I happen to be in the area, say a week from now, I would see your place probably all furnished then, wouldn't I?"

Gambardella's henchman casually walked to the fireplace mantle, and lifted a photo mounted there.

"Nice looking kids. Is this your son and your daughter? They must be teenagers right about now. Hopefully, they're in good health. Teenagers today can be pretty wild and do crazy things. You wouldn't want them to get hurt out there in any way, what with all the accidents involving teenagers."

"Mr. Trout, we don't mean to alarm you or Mrs. Trout in any way. I just need to pay a debt to my former employee, but I can't seem to find him."

"I wish I could help you, Mr. Gambardella, but we haven't heard a word from Richie since we bought the furniture. We don't know where he is."

Gambardella and his goon said goodbye to the Trouts and headed for the front door. As he walked out the front door, he turned to Claude Trout.

"Really nice looking kids you've got, Mr. Trout. Keep them safe. It's a tough world out there."

Once they were gone, Claude turned to his wife and said, "Richie did tell us they might be by. Are you okay?" he asked looking at his concerned wife.

His wife gave him an unconvincing shrug as she answered, "I hope we don't see him again, he scares me."

CHAPTER 17

THE APARTMENT

Following an absolutely wonderful three days in Pittsburg with Sydney, Drew walked into his office at Assurance in the late morning on Friday. He talked to Art Donnelly, his assistant, and wondered if there was any more news on the burglar case they were tracking. Drew knew all too well that he could delay payment on the pearls to the Conways for only so long before they would start to file a complaint with the company, or even worse, complain to the insurance commissioner for the State of Rhode Island.

"This Carol Simonton woman from Simonton Jewelry at the mall called, and your secretary passed the call on to me. She wanted us to know that the mall also had outside cameras, not only at the exit doors, but throughout the parking areas related to each exit. She said it might be worth it for us to take a look at their tapes from the day the woman tried to fence the pearls at her store."

"Sure, what do we have to lose? Do you want to take a ride?" Drew asked.

"I can't today. I'm wrapping up another case right now, and I need to get the paperwork done so I can close the file by the weekend," Donnelly answered.

"I'll take a ride over there myself then."

His mind clearly wasn't on work that day, and he and Sydney were meeting later for cocktails at Adeline's in Cumberland, and dinner afterwards at Andrew's Bistro. When he arrived at the Emerald Square Mall, he asked one of the guards how to get to the security office where they kept video records of the entire mall. The guard directed him to the second floor of the mall to offices tucked into the northern corner, near the Sears store, one of the anchor stores. Following the usual introductions as he confronted a clerk at the security window, the head of security appeared from a rear office.

"May I ask why you need to see videos from our cameras? Was there a crime that I am not aware of?"

"No, not exactly. But we have reason to believe that a woman tried to fence stolen jewelry at Simonton's earlier this month. We have their video, which doesn't tell us a whole lot, but we heard from Ms. Simonton that you have cameras at all the exits, and even some in the parking areas. If this is the case, I'd like to look at your footage from ten a.m. to noon on Monday, January twenty-eighth for all exits. If we spot her leaving a particular exit, maybe we can look at where that exit leads to."

"Mr. Diamond, normally we don't allow anyone but the police to have access to our security system. Are the police aware of this person you are talking about?"

"If you call Detective Jack Mullen of the North Attleboro police, he'll verify who I am, and he's fully aware of
my involvement in this case. He's been working on several
burglaries in the area, and this woman could very well
be responsible for all of them. But if you won't allow my
company to review the videos, I'll just have to come back
with Jack. We're both working on this, but for different
reasons. In my case, if my company can retrieve most of
the stolen jewelry, we won't have to dish out thousands
of dollars to victims, but only if we recover their jewelry."

"That won't be necessary, Mr. Diamond. I understand what you're saying. Follow me, please."

The long corridor led to a corner room the size of a
large conference room. There were no less than fifty cameras in the room, all specific to a particular location in the
mall. In addition, there were ten cameras in the various
parking lots and garages throughout the mall. The cameras did not require any personal monitoring, and the
room was empty of any people.

"Okay, let's start with the second floor exits for the
time you want. If we don't see this person leaving the mall
this way, then she left from the ground floor. The third
floor cameras might catch someone going out the roof of
the mall, but we can check that one last."

The security officer went from monitor to monitor
for the second floor, and came up with nothing on the
first five monitors. But on the sixth monitor, there she
was, a clear image of a woman with the same description
as the one on the jewelry store tape. The exit she used

led to the parking garage at the rear of the mall. Next he walked to a monitor which displayed activity in that parking garage. He entered the hourly search parameters in that garage and watched as the blonde woman, now wearing sunglasses, made her way toward the rows of parked cars, until she was out of sight. Five minutes later, an SUV drove past the camera and out the garage exit. The driver was a dark haired figure, hard to identify because of the tinted windshields on the SUV, and the poor garage lighting.

"Run it again. Let's see if we can make out the make and model of the vehicle, and maybe get a glimpse of the license plate," Drew told the security officer.

"The camera has a poor angle for the plate number, but it looks like a Toyota RAV4, the kind with the spare tire mounted on the outside back of the SUV, rather than under the floor on the inside. The glare on the plate makes the number unreadable, but there is a dealer name there...Boch Toyota."

"This may not be the car. The driver of this car was clearly not blonde, or was she?" Drew shouted. "Can you get me a copy of this tape? And include up to fifteen minutes after this vehicle was seen leaving the garage. She could have exited later than this car."

"Or she could have avoided the loop to exit the garage if she was parked way at the other end," the security officer blurted out.

"What do you mean?"

"At the very bottom of that row of cars, it's easier just to catch the exit from there. You don't need to make the loop to get to the same exit."

"So, you're saying we may never see the vehicle leaving if it was parked at the lower end, and it went directly out the exit."

"That's right. Come on, I'll show you what I mean."

They walked the short distance to the exit in question, and Drew saw what the security officer meant. And there were no cameras directly at the exit from the garage. He thanked the officer for his help, and headed for Adeline's. It was now nearly four o'clock in the afternoon, the time they said they would meet. He arrived at ten minutes to four, and decided to wait in his car until Sydney arrived. His car was parked in the left corner of the lot outside Adeline's, barely visible with several cars parked next to his. Friday afternoon cocktail hours were more common than not, as workers of all kinds welcomed the arrival of the weekend with a drink or two at their favorite watering hole.

At four o'clock, Sydney pulled up in her Toyota RAV4 and entered the tavern. Drew got out of his car, and walked toward her car. The rear of the SUV had the spare tire mounted on the outside of the vehicle, and the dealer name "Boch Toyota" was imprinted on the left side near the spare tire.

Suddenly, he began to have doubts again as to who Sydney Malone really was. This was the third coincidence between Sydney and the burglar. He would be cautious at how he handled this series of similarities.

"Hey, Drew, did you just pull up? I just got here myself. Business is picking up. Spring is right around the corner, and it seems people are getting ready to buy and sell. I picked up three clients today. Obviously this means we'll have to go back to New Hampshire for another three days. The time up there seems to have been lucky for me, in more ways than one," she stated as she kissed him on the cheek and signaled the waitress over to their corner table.

"Are you working tomorrow?" he asked.

"I have a closing from twelve to two, and a showing at three. Why do you ask?"

"There's a basketball game at the "Dunk" from twelve to about four...two games actually. It seems my company is one of the tournament sponsors for the NCAA regionals over there, and I was going to ask you to go with me."

"Sorry, but I'll be ready at six for dinner at Capriccio's and the theatre afterwards."

"No problem. Art's been after me to go to the games with him anyway. Now I won't have to worry about him for a while."

Drew had no such tickets to a basketball game. Instead, he planned on going to Sydney's apartment just before noon, using his lock picking expertise to enter her apartment when she was gone. He didn't know what he'd find, but he was now suspicious at this string of similarities with the burglar.

He parked his car in the medical lot across the street from the entrance to the Chimney Hill Apartments at eleven fifteen on Saturday morning. At eleven thirty, Sydney's car left the complex and headed supposedly to her office in Smithfield. Drew left the medical lot and drove up the entrance to Chimney Hill, and parked his car away from the main entrance. He punched in the three-digit number Sydney had given him to enter the apartment building. He then took the stairs to the fifth floor. As he opened the stairwell door, he looked both ways to be sure no one was there. He then quickly pulled out his case of small tools to open a locked door, and within seconds he was safely inside her apartment as he relocked the door.

He decided to start browsing carefully through her bedroom. Knowing how tidy the burglar was in the thefts from homes, Drew made certain he replaced items exactly the way they were in her drawers and closets.

Suddenly, he heard the sound of a key turning in the door, and the door slamming shut. He quickly entered the bedroom closet with sliding doors, and quietly slid the door closed. Sydney had forgotten to take her laptop from the kitchen counter, and retrieved it. A minute later, Drew heard the door closing again. He cautiously slid the closet door open, and peered out from the bedroom area. There was no one there.

As he re-entered the bedroom, the open closet door showed a black duffle bag on the top shelf. He carefully removed the bag and placed it on the floor as he unzipped it open. He noticed a black baseball cap, a pair of black leather gloves, a pair of spandex leotards, and black sneakers. He closed the bag, and returned it to its spot on the shelf. *Okay, Sydney, what have you done?* He pondered. Within minutes, he was out of the apartment and back in his car.

CHAPTER 18

THE TRASH

Sydney's doorbell rang at five fifteen as Drew stood at the door to number 510. In less than a minute, she opened the door, and had him sit in the living room for a minute while she finished adding her jewelry in front of the bedroom mirror.

"It's about thirty minutes to Capriccio's, so we're okay for our six o'clock reservation. Providence is bustling though with that basketball tournament in town. The restaurants will be packed tonight. This is a great weekend for them. Crowded dining in March in Rhode Island seldom happens."

He had remembered to tune in to ESPN Sports Center before he left his apartment in Lincoln, to make sure he got the names of the four teams playing that afternoon at the Dunk. If Sydney should ask, he could talk as if he actually was at the games, not that he expected her to ask…basketball wasn't exactly her game.

After dinner, they were walking over to the Providence Performing Arts Center to see *The Phantom of the Opera* at eight. That gave them two hours to spend at Capriccio's, more than ample time for what he had in mind.

Sydney appeared in a black dress and, ironically, wearing a white pearl necklace. She looked ravishing as she grabbed her black winter coat from the hallway closet and handed it to Drew. He held it open as she slipped one arm and then the other over a white satin scarf covering her entire neckline. She grabbed her purse and, with her short black hair combed perfectly, they headed out the door. She placed her arm under his as they made their way to the elevator and down to his car parked out front.

Twenty minutes later, he pulled into the valet parking station in front of the restaurant.

"Jimmy, we're going over to PPAC afterwards. Can you keep my car in the lot until about ten?"

"No problem, Mr. Diamond. I'll have your car warmed up by ten."

"Well, Mr. Bigshot, I guess you've been here more than once before," she said as the valet opened her car door.

They entered the restaurant and climbed down the staircase to the lower level dining room. The cobblestone floor had several coats of polish, and still looked good after many years. The fireplace was blazing with firewood, and the aroma of burning timbers emanated through the large open dining area. Drew believed that the large open space concept of this dining room had much more ambiance than some of the smaller private dining tables surrounding the bar area.

The waiter approached with menus in hand, and took their cocktail order. Drew looked at his watch, and saw that it wasn't yet six o'clock.

"We've got plenty of time, so let's enjoy the drinks, and maybe a side of calamari before we order."

"What's wrong, Drew, you seem a bit edgy tonight? Something on your mind?" she asked.

"Well, now that you ask, this burglary case has me puzzled. Maybe you can help?" he asked.

"I don't know how, but fire away," she answered somewhat cautiously.

"Okay, here's what I have so far. We know the burglar is about five six, has a bruise on the right leg from a dog bite, has a small tattoo on the neck, and likely drives a Toyota SUV."

"How do you know all that? Wow, that's a far cry from the first time you mentioned the case. We're still talking about the pearls, right?"

"We, Detective Mullen and I, watched a video from one of the houses that was broken into, and made out a figure running from the back yard grabbing the right leg. Then one of the jewelry stores at the mall had a video of a blonde woman trying to fence the pearls there. We couldn't make out the face on these videos, but did notice a tattoo on the right side of the neck, kind of like your little one there. Then we went to security at the mall, and their cameras showed the blonde leaving the mall by a rear exit to the parking garage, and a Toyota

SUV pulling out a few minutes later. That might not actually be the burglar's vehicle, because I found out that customers can drive out the exit from the far end of the garage, where there are no cameras. And this SUV had tinted windshields making it impossible to see who was driving. The angle of the lights in the garage also made it impossible to get a license plate."

Sydney did not look up from her cocktail glass as she took several sips rather quickly.

"Are you with me on this? I've got a lot of clues, but nothing definite. I could probably use the burglar's clothing added to the mix to make it all the more convincing, but I'll have to find it first. Then if everything else matches, I might be on to something," he said as he stared directly at Sydney.

She didn't know how to react. She simply stared back at him in silence until he spoke again.

"Here's where maybe you can help me."

"And how is that?" she asked sheepishly.

"Let's just suppose for a minute you were a burglar, and you had these pearls you had to get rid of, not knowing if they were cheap or not, or even worth fencing. Chances are though, because they were under clothing in a woman's bureau, they're worth something. Using your woman's intuition and knowledge of this area more than I have, where would you go to get rid of these pearls, hypothetically, that is?" he asked, still staring directly at her.

She sat there, holding her cocktail glass with both hands for a moment, before she replied.

Does he know I'm the one? Is this his subtle way of telling me that he knows?

"If I had any kind of jewelry that I owned, and wanted to sell, the only place I can think of is at a jewelry store. Who else buys jewelry? Maybe in New York there are wholesale places, I don't know, I've never been to one. But for that matter, I don't own expensive stuff anyway. Places like Simonton Jewelers at the mall come to mind, Baxter's, Jared's, and even a Providence one like Hunter Jewelers, or Ross Simon in Warwick. But, wouldn't they ask for identification of some sort?"

"That's true. They're supposed to ask for proof that you're the rightful owner, but what if the jewelry was handed down to you by someone? In this case, the woman who had insurance on the pearls also had a copy of the estate settlement from her mother's estate, showing the pearls as part of her will. But not all jewelers are that picky. And some are downright dishonest, and out to make a quick buck. I'll probably check out Hunters and Ross Simon on Monday. Maybe their camera footage will show something."

The calamari appetizer arrived, and the conversation soon shifted.

"Did you start having the walls painted in your new place?" she asked.

"Actually, they'll be done on Monday. And the carpet guy comes on Thursday. I've got carpet samples in the car. Maybe you can help me pick out a good one tomorrow? We can take a ride to the condo, and match some carpet samples against the walls that are already painted."

"Sure, but not in the morning. It's bad enough I had to be in the office today before noon. Sunday is the only day this week I get to sleep in, and I've got to tell you, I'm exhausted. It's been a long day."

"Let's order dinner while we do this appetizer. That way, we can take our time with dinner until the show."

Dinner was fairly quiet, and by seven thirty they were sipping cappuccinos before leaving for PPAC. The musical was excellent and seemed to calm Sydney down. Drew, on the other hand, was as vocal as at the restaurant. She didn't quite know how to react to any of his questions or comments, worried that she somehow would implicate herself by accident.

When they arrived at her apartment building, she simply gave him a kiss, and stated again how tired she was, and that she was going straight to bed. He watched as she entered the building without once turning around. His message had been delivered, painful as it was. But would he even accuse her directly? This was a dilemma he had to wrestle with.

On Sunday morning, Drew, a Roman Catholic, attended the ten o'clock Mass at St. Ambrose Church in Albion, only one mile from his apartment. Albion was part of the town of Lincoln, and St. Ambrose Church had been an integral part of this village for over a hundred years. Following the service, he returned home around eleven. As he entered his apartment, he noticed the blinking light from his answering machine. He pressed the recall button.

"Hi, Drew. I'm afraid I'm going to have to pass on

going to your condo this afternoon. I'm nursing a huge migraine, and I'm going to stay in bed for a few more hours. I hope I'm not coming down with something. I'll call you later this week. Have a wonderful day."

Oh, Sydney, Sydney, what are we going to do?

At one o'clock in the afternoon, Sydney's so-called migraine had long left her head as she pondered how to approach Drew, if at all, about these burglaries. Her first thought was to get rid of her black outfit that she wore during the break-ins. As she retrieved the duffel bag from her bedroom closet, she noticed that the zipper on top of the bag was not fully closed. In Sydney's mind, if it had a zipper, it should be fully closed, whether on her purse, her gym bag, or the zipper bag carrying her laptop. She was sure she had fully zipped it closed the last time she used it.

Inside the bag, everything appeared in order, but the open zipper bothered her. Nonetheless, she emptied the contents into a brown trash bag, and tied the bag closed. When she brought the trash bag out of the bedroom and placed it next to her apartment door, she noticed a white envelope on the floor just inside the door. She picked it up, it had no writing on the envelope, and was unsealed.

I know you are the burglar the police are looking for. I will not reveal who you are to them if you tell me where you fenced the jewelry…especially the pearls. I will not tell Drew Diamond or Detective Jack Mullen. I just need to know who you fenced them to. Leave the name under your windshield wiper on the driver's side of your car no later than nine tonight. Otherwise, I will take what I know to the police.

She thought about who would leave such a message. Could it be one of the oil servicemen who somehow found out who she was? Or was it a police trap because the case was going nowhere at the moment? Or could it be Drew himself using this angle to get to her? The dinner conversation the night before sure made it seem like he, too, wanted to know where one would fence these pearls.

But she trusted Drew. Their relationship had grown significantly in the last few weeks, and she feared losing the only man she had grown close to since her husband died ten years earlier.

It is what it is, she pondered. She had made a decision to stop doing any further break-ins, and to somehow return all of the stolen cash to her victims over time. Although it wouldn't be a total retribution, it was a gesture of atonement.

She took the elevator to the first floor, and walked out the rear door of the building. She advanced toward the huge trash bin, carrying the brown trash bag containing her black outfit, and tossed the bag into the bin. No one was around, or so she thought, as she re-entered the building. She looked at her watch as she rode the elevator back to her apartment. Once there, she picked up the phone and called Drew. As Drew's phone rang, he noticed Sydney's name appear on his screen.

"Hi, are you feeling better?"

"Wow, those few hours more of sleep really did the trick. Do you still want to go over those rug samples at the condo?"

"That would be great. Can you meet me there around three?" he asked.

"I'll be there. I can't seem to get enough of you, Drew Diamond."

"Likewise, Sydney."

At three o'clock, she rang the doorbell to the condo, although she couldn't see Drew's car parked out front. Within a minute, he opened the door and greeted her with a kiss on the cheek.

"Where's your car?" she asked.

"It's parked in front of the garage out back. I thought I'd start bringing some things over in my car," he answered.

As she entered the condo and heard Drew's comment, her eyes naturally shifted to the rear of the condo. On the floor, near the back door to the garage, sat a brown trash bag, neatly closed and tied with a red strap. She was stunned when she saw the trash bag.

"Looks like you've been doing some cleaning," she uttered, pointing to the trash bag.

"Oh, that, no, it's not me. That must be junk from the painter. He probably didn't know where the trash bins are, so he just left it there for me to dump."

The rest of the afternoon was spent going over carpet samples to match the new wall color. By five o'clock, they were done.

"I'd ask you to dinner tonight, but I'm off to Narragansett for Junior's birthday with Claire. I'll call you during the week. Oh, by the way, thanks for the tips on jewelry stores last night. I'll be visiting some tomorrow, and see where it goes."

Ten minutes later, Sydney was back at her apartment. Rather than taking the elevator upstairs, she went out the back door of the building and made a beeline towards the trash bins, using the flashlight from her glove compartment in the car. She could reach the opening to the bin by propping herself up onto a small ledge at the bottom of the bin. There were no brown trash bags in sight like the one she had tossed in earlier. She raced back into the building, took the elevator to the fifth floor, and ran to her apartment, fumbling for the apartment key. Once inside, she hurried to the kitchen island, and grabbed a set of keys, and ran out the door.

Within five minutes, she reached Drew's condo, making sure his car was no longer parked in front of his garage at the rear of the condo. She carefully entered the condo, using the key she still had to enter when she was having showings of the condo. She flipped on the light switch, and looked toward the back door. There was no trash bag anywhere.

The look on her face said it all! She raced back to her apartment, grabbed a piece of paper from the pad on the kitchen counter, and wrote two words, *Hunter Jewelry.* She then rode the elevator down to the main floor and slipped the folded paper under the windshield wiper on the driver's side. She looked all around her to see if anyone was watching, but it was pitch dark, and she saw no one or nothing unusual.

When she left for work on Monday morning, the note was no longer under the windshield wiper.

CHAPTER 19

CLARKSVILLE

On Monday morning, Richie walked to the counter in the Woodbury Food Court at the university. To his surprise, he was greeted by another woman instead of Gloria.

"What can I get for you this morning, sir?" the elderly lady asked.

"Where's Gloria today? I hope she isn't sick or anything? There's a lot of flu running around these days."

"I don't know who Gloria is, sir. I'm just filling in. You're better off asking the woman at the cash register. Maybe she can help you."

"How about two eggs over lightly and two wheat toasts."

He slid his tray along the buffet track on the counter toward the cashier.

"Good morning, Richie. How are you today?" the woman asked.

"Can you tell me where Gloria is today? Did she have vacation time? I hope she isn't sick?"

"She left a message on her supervisor's phone early this morning. Something about an emergency with her mother back home. Marge was nice enough to fill in for Gloria."

"Do you know what happened to her mom?

"The super said she was rushed to the hospital in Colebrook, New Hampshire in the middle of the night. Maybe a heart attack."

Throughout the day, all he could think about was Gloria. She didn't need any bad news. Living alone had been very lonely for her, and getting a phone call in the early hours of the morning, informing her of an emergency a hundred forty miles away, wouldn't help. Like Sydney, Gloria finally was beginning to have a life again. Sure it had only been one date, but the afternoons at the coffee shop with Richie were almost daily now, and she and Richie were getting much closer.

At three o'clock sharp, as soon as his shift was done at the athletic complex, he went straight to the administrative office and asked the secretary for a favor.

"Jenny, I need to get to a hospital in Colebrook, New Hampshire today. I don't even know where Colebrook is, let alone how far away it is. Can you look it up for me on the computer?"

"Sure, let's see, that would be the Upper Connecticut Valley Hospital, 181 Corliss Lane. It's one hundred thirty three miles from here. You take Maine Route 26 north to New Hampshire 26 west. Is everything all right with you?"

"Oh, yes, I need to visit a friend whose mom is hospitalized there. Thank you for asking."

He jumped in his car and headed for Colebrook, not knowing exactly what he'd find when he got there. He had called his mother to tell her he would not be home for dinner. She expressed concern for Gloria's mother, and asked Richie to call her with any news.

He followed the route directions Jenny had given him. The rural roads were windy and slow-moving. Two and a half hours later, and in the dark, he arrived at the hospital and went to the desk in the emergency room.

"Pardon me, Ma'am, you brought in a woman from Clarksville early this morning, last name would be Jones. Can you tell me where she is?" he asked with a concerned look on his face.

"Are you a relative, sir?" she asked.

"No, I am a friend of her daughter Gloria."

At that moment, Ralph Jones was walking by on his way to the cafeteria when he heard the name Gloria.

"Excuse me, you know my daughter Gloria, Gloria Sokoloski?"

"Yes, I'm Richie Lamb. We both work at the university in Portland."

"I'm her father. She's with her mother right now. I'll take you to her."

"Mrs. Jones, is she okay?" Richie asked very seriously.

"Thankfully, yes. She had a slight heart attack early this morning, but the doctors think the worst is over. But she'll need some care for a while at home."

They reached the intensive care unit on the second

floor, and Ralph Jones led Richie to his wife's room. As he entered, Gloria looked up from her chair at her mother's bedside.

"Richie, what are you doing here?" she asked loudly as she jumped from the chair and ran to him, reaching for his hands with both of hers.

"I was worried about you and your mom. I wanted to make sure you were okay."

"You have got to be kidding me. You drove all the way up here to make sure I was alright? That's nearly a three-hour drive. How did you know where to find me?" she asked with an elated look on her face.

"The secretary at the administrative office said this was the only hospital in Colebrook. So here I am."

"My mom is okay, just gave us quite a scare though. Come on over, I'll introduce you," she replied as she led him closer to her mother's bed.

"I'm happy to meet you, Mrs. Jones. You have a wonderful daughter. We work at the same university in Portland."

Ralph Jones excused himself as he left to return to the cafeteria on the ground level to get a bite to eat, while Gloria and Richie stayed with Mrs. Jones. Thirty minutes later, Ralph returned, and told Gloria and Richie that they should do the same. It was nearly seven o'clock, and he didn't know how long they would be serving warm food. Fortunately, they made it there before the cafeteria section serving dinners was closing. Gloria could still not believe he had driven all the way to Colebrook after work.

"Lucky for me, there is no snow on the ground any more. So the roads are in good shape. But I wouldn't want to be stuck up here after a snowstorm."

"Well, my hometown of Clarksville is about eleven miles north of here, so I know what you mean. Let's order something. I can see the women behind the counter are anxious to put all the food away for tonight."

Their dinner was on a plate on a tray, not exactly the fine dining experience of DiMillo's On The Water back in Portland, but it didn't matter to either of them. They stayed there for nearly an hour and a half until Gloria glanced at her watch.

"We had better get back up, my father will wonder what happened to us."

When they entered the hospital room, Ralph was talking to one of the nurses, and he turned to them.

"The hospital says I can stay here with her through the night, if I want to. Why don't you take Richie here to the house, and he can stay overnight there. The roads are not lit very well at night, and the colder the temperature gets during the night, the more the roads are likely to ice up. You couldn't get back to Portland until way after eleven at the earliest."

"That's very nice of you to offer, sir, but I don't want to put you out. You both have a lot more on your mind than having to worry about me. I'll be fine."

"No, my dad's right, you have no idea how bad the roads get once the temperature drops below freezing up here. Call your mother, so she doesn't worry, and stay at our house tonight, period," Gloria added.

Richie's mother was pleased he wouldn't be driving home so late from a long distance away. She smiled at the news he would be staying overnight at Gloria's parents' home. He followed Gloria to Clarksville. It was now nearly nine o'clock, and both had had a long day. Gloria showed him to the guest room, while she would sleep across the hall in the master bedroom for the night.

Before he went to bed, Richie walked downstairs to get a glass of water. As he drank his water, he walked into the living room and noticed pictures on the mantle of the fireplace. Several showed Gloria as a teenager, some with a girlfriend. He finished his water and walked back upstairs.

He closed the door to the bedroom, undressed, and got into bed in only his underwear and undershirt. Gloria had brought him one of her father's bathrobes if he needed to go downstairs during the night. The light switch was near the bed, and he could reach it without getting up. There was a night light in the hallway that shined slightly under his bedroom door.

"Richie, can I come in?" the voice from outside his bedroom door murmured.

Without waiting for a reply, Gloria opened the door and stood there in her nightgown, shaking like a leaf. Richie, about to doze off, groggily got up and went to her. She was shivering uncontrollably. He quickly wrapped his arms around her, and held her tightly against his body. He then reached for the robe at the foot of the bed, and wrapped it around both of them.

"I'm afraid, Richie. I nearly lost her today. I never

realized how much she meant to me, but now, after all these years, we were getting so close to each other again."

"It's okay, just breathe deeply and warm up. I'm here."

"It's been a long time since I was in the arms of any-one alone."

"Well, I don't know about that, but I've never been with anyone before at all," he said.

"Can I stay with you tonight? I don't want to go back to my room. Besides, this is my room, or at least it was for many years."

"What you need right now is a good night's sleep. If you trust me not to jump you during the night, then stay. But the next time we're in the same bedroom at night, I can't promise anything."

She smiled and calmed down as they entered the bed and covered themselves in the two quilts on the bed. Within five minutes, they were both sound asleep. The following morning, when Gloria woke, Richie was gone. She put on a robe and hurried down the staircase. Richie had already showered and shaved in the downstairs bath-room, and had a cup of coffee in his hands.

"Good morning. I hope I didn't snore. You were, like, out of it and didn't budge all night. Did you sleep well?"

"I never heard a peep, and I'm a lousy sleeper. Are you sure you didn't drug me last night, and take advan-tage of me?"

"I'll never tell. I've got to go back to Portland. I think maybe you want to spend some time this week with your mom. Take some vacation time and stay up here this week. I'll call you later this afternoon."

She walked up to him and, without hesitation, kissed him on the lips for what seemed a minute. He looked at her, and then kissed her right back.

"You are the best thing that's happened to me, Gloria Sokoloski. Where have you been all my life?"

*   *   *

"I'm planning on going back to Pittsburg on Friday morning until Sunday afternoon. Can you get away this weekend?" Drew asked as he called Sydney on Tuesday morning.

"Uh, let me check my schedule, and get back to you later today," she answered on her cell phone.

Was this going to be the final confrontation between the two? Was Drew going to directly accuse her of being the burglar he sought? She thought about his cabin being the perfect private setting for such a confrontation. She had to know what he was thinking. She wanted this to be over. She was genuinely sorry she had ever resorted to burglarizing homes to pay for her elevated lifestyle. Unfortunately, she had not yet been as successful in the real estate sales business to spend as much as she did. She promised herself she would make changes in her lifestyle, and live within her income going forward.

Sydney decided to face the music, and told Drew later that day of her decision.

"I can leave on Friday morning any time."

"Great. How about eight in the morning again?"

On Tuesday afternoon, Drew called Ralph Jones and

left a message that he would be at the cabin from Friday afternoon through Sunday after lunch, and could he make sure all the utilities were working properly, and that there was ample firewood for the weekend.

After the phone call, he drove to Providence, and walked into Hunter Jewelry on Dorrance Street. He walked up to the gentleman at the counter.

"Are you the owner?"

"Yes, I'm Garrett Hunter. How can I help you?"

"My name is Drew Diamond and I'm an investigator for Assurance Property & Casualty Insurance. About a week or two ago, I emailed you a photo of a string of pearls and a matching ring that had been stolen, with a request to notify me if anyone attempted to sell them here. Do you recall that email, Mr. Hunter?"

"Yes, I do remember. As a matter of fact, I have it right here in this folder," he replied as he reached under the counter. "But I can't say that I've seen anyone come in here to sell them though."

"As all jewelry stores have, I'm sure you have cameras throughout your store. Is that right?"

"Yes, of course we do. Why do you ask?"

"We have a suspect, Detective Mullen of the North Attleboro Police and I, that we believe may have attempted to sell the pearls at different jewelry stores in the area. She appeared on a video in North Attleboro. Could I see your footage from Monday and Tuesday from two weeks ago, just in case she may have come in here when you weren't working the counter?"

Garrett was surprised at this request, never expecting

anyone to want to review his video tapes. Like a fool, he had paid no attention to the fact that the blonde woman would appear on tape more than once. He needed to come up with an excuse quickly to delay showing any tapes to Drew, so that he could erase them. *How could I have been so careless?* he thought.

"My system is down right now, but if you come back tomorrow, it should be back up and running. I'm installing more cameras in the ceiling vents, and the software guy needed to shut the system down while he added the new camera connections," Garrett replied unconvincingly.

"Oh, really! I'm kind of a software geek myself. Maybe I can take a look for you. That way, I can save the need to come back. I've got several other stores to go to."

"I can't let you do that. I have no idea what you know about my security cameras, and I certainly can't allow you to fool around with them."

"I'll tell you what, why don't I call Detective Mullen right now, and have him bring his computer expert with him. I'm certain he's very qualified to retrieve the tapes I'm looking for without disturbing your system at all," Drew stated as he started to punch Mullen's number on his cell phone.

"That won't be necessary. What exactly is it that you're looking for, Mr. Diamond?"

"It's quite simple really, Mr. Hunter. My company may be on the hook to pay a $100,000 claim for these pearls if they're not found and returned to their owner. If by chance, the person who fenced them happened to do it here, hypothetically, you or someone else would get rid of them as quickly as you can, and for a decent profit from what you paid for them. Correct me if I'm wrong, please. And my guess is they're long gone from this area by now, probably New York. Should these pearls somehow land on my desk, say within the next two days, and your tapes suddenly disappear, our business would be done, wouldn't it?"

"You're bluffing, Mr. Diamond, and you have no proof whatsoever as to what's on those tapes," Garrett replied with a sneer on his face.

"Mr. Hunter, the woman you dealt with has been cornered, and she will testify, if she has to, that she sold the pearls to you. I don't know who you sold them to, but I want them back. If you do that, I'll forget I ever was here. But, if you don't get them back, and they're not on my desk by late Thursday, I will hand the tapes over to Detective Mullen. Do you know how much time you'll do for fencing $100,000 pearls, Mr. Hunter? Who will take care of your family while you're in prison? Inside my suit jacket is a holster which carries a nine millimeter pistol. You will lead me to your security monitor, and give me the tapes I'm looking for, and you will do it now."

Drew's former police tactics of intimidating a criminal during interrogations were true to form on this occasion.

"When the pearls are on my desk in a manila envelope addressed to me, the tapes will be returned to you on Saturday morning by courier. Are we clear on this?" he emphasized with a glare in his eyes. "Now, let's look at those tapes, shall we?"

Garrett was boxed in a corner, and he realized it. He

locked the door to the store, hung a sign stating he would return in ten minutes, and proceeded to unlock his office door. After viewing the videos, Drew removed the tapes of the ones he needed, and turned to Garrett.

"Mr. Hunter, remember, no later than Thursday night. Here's my card, in case you get lost finding my office," he softly said as he left the store, after unlocking the front door.

The call to Brynn McDaniel in New York would be a costly one. Fortunately, the pearls were retrievable, but unfortunately, for the price of $50,000, to which he agreed. Late Monday afternoon, he left a text message on Richie's phone. *Waldo is needed urgently to pick up a package at the same location he brought the first delivery. Can you meet me in Hopkinton on Tuesday at six o'clock after work?*

Richie made arrangements at the university to take the day off on Thursday, citing medical treatment for his mother. Since he had not accrued enough time to qualify for paid vacation time, he needed to take the day off without pay. At six o'clock on Tuesday, he entered the 110 Grill, and Garrett was sitting at the bar.

"Glad you could make it, Richie. This trip to Brynn's is crucial. You must give him the briefcase as before. In return, he will return the briefcase to you after placing something in it. I'll be back here on Thursday afternoon at two. Try to get here as fast as you can . I can only give you $1,000 this time. I hope you still will do this for me?" he pleaded.

"Garrett, you got me a fresh start, and things are looking up for me right now. I owe you for doing this.

But after this one, I can't do it anymore. I want to make a clean break from anything outside the law."

"You know, Richie, right about now, I hear what you're saying, and I may stop doing this myself. I've got too much to lose. If I ever get arrested for dealing in stolen property, my family and my life would go up in smoke."

Richie followed the same pattern in his second trip to New York as he did the first time. After making the exchange in Brynn's office, he held onto the briefcase as if his life depended on it. Little did he know it was actually Garrett's future life that depended on it. He arrived in Hopkinton at three in the afternoon on Thursday, and Garrett was at the bar. He had just called Gloria on her cell phone.

"Hi, I was hoping I could go up to Clarksville after work tomorrow. I could be there around six, and we could go out to dinner," he had said when she answered the phone.

"What a wonderful idea. I've missed seeing you this week, but I did get to spend a lot of time with my mom. That was precious. She's doing much better, and my dad finally had a chance to get some work done with me around to care for her. I'll be going back home to Portland on Sunday. Are you sure you want to drive all the way up here just to take me out to dinner?"

"My mom is having dinner with our landlord on the second floor. They wanted me to go, too, but I'd rather be with you, if that's alright?"

"Are you kidding? I'll be ready when you get here. Do you remember how to get to our house?"

"Not a problem. See you at six."

The exchange with Garrett went as planned. Garrett opened the briefcase in front of Richie, and exhaled a huge sigh at seeing the contents. He then reached into his suit jacket, and plopped an envelope on the counter, sliding it in front of Richie.

"Not this time, Garrett. You've done enough for me," he said as he slid the envelope back towards Garrett. "I think it's time I made a clean break, and now is as good as ever. Put the money to good use. Be thankful for your wife, your kids, your health, and your freedom. Someday, I hope to have all those myself. It's been a pleasure, Garrett. I don't think we'll be seeing each other again."

CHAPTER 20

THE CABIN

The trip to Pittsburg on Friday morning was pretty quiet for about an hour until Drew spoke.

"Do you remember that burglary case I was talking about, the one involving those expensive pearls?" he asked.

"How can I forget? You've been talking about it almost every time we're together. Anything new?"

"As a matter of fact, yes, a lot has happened since I visited Hunter Jewelry on Monday. I received a tip that their video would show that he bought them off the blonde. I convinced him to either tell me who he sold them to, or get them back to me this week."

"And, what happened?" she asked eagerly waiting for an answer.

"Let's just say that the owner will have her pearls back in exchange for the video tapes Mr. Hunter I'm sure has erased by now. I hope the woman burglar we're looking for doesn't continue doing this. She's going to get caught one day, and likely will face a lot of jail time. I'm hoping she quits while she's ahead of the game. We are very close to catching her. If Mullen had her burglary outfit added to the videos we already have, I think he could come up with a few suspects. There haven't been any new break-ins in the last two weeks. That's a good sign. And my company doesn't have to dish out $100,000. Now that's cause for celebration."

"Oh, no, another celebration," she blurted out, exhaling a sigh of relief.

*   *   *

The weather in Portland was pouring rain. April had arrived, and with it came two straight days of rain. Richie's boss had hoped to fertilize the baseball field, and do other outside work, but the amount of rain had drenched the field. Richie suggested to his boss that he could do the job on Sunday when the weather would be better in exchange for leaving early on Friday. His boss agreed, and Richie began the drive to Clarksville shortly before noon. He arrived at Gloria's house at two-thirty in the afternoon. Gloria smiled as she answered the doorbell.

In the meantime, the telephone rang at the Jones residence, and Ralph answered.

"Ralph, Drew Diamond. Didn't you get my message earlier this week?

"Oh, I'm sorry, Mr. Diamond. We had a medical crisis here with Mrs. Jones, and I haven't been home much.

She's back home now, and I'm just seeing the message on the answering machine," he answered rubbing his hair in disbelief.

"Right now, there's no heat, no chopped wood, and the cabin could use a sprucing up. Is it possible for you or somebody to get over here to help get some of these things done? Is Mrs. Jones okay enough for you to leave her alone for a while?"

"I'll be right over, Mr. Diamond," he replied.

Ralph Jones was exhausted from the activities of the week, and Gloria was worried that this additional work would be more than he could handle all at once.

"I'll go with you, Mr. Jones," Richie said as he could see the anguish on his face.

"Why don't you all go. The three of you can probably get all of this done in an hour or so. I'll be fine. I don't need anything, and I'll have the phone next to me here in the living room," Mrs. Jones said as she looked at the three of them.

"It's up to you, Gloria. Your father has had a rough week, and I have no problem helping out. I'm not sure you need to come anyway," Richie said.

"And leave you and my father to do the cleaning inside the cabin. You guys handle the wood and the heat in the cabin, and I'll get the inside done in no time," she answered.

Ralph was not about to refuse the help. They left in Ralph's pickup truck and arrived at the cabin within ten minutes. Drew and Sydney were unloading their overnight luggage from the trunk of Drew's car as the pickup truck parked near the side of the cabin.

"Here, let me help you bring some of that stuff in the cabin," Richie shouted as he neared Drew's car.

"Oh, hello, I don't think we've met," Drew said as he extended his hand to Ritchie.

"I'm Drew Diamond."

"Nice to meet you, Mr. Diamond. I'm Richie Lamb. I understand you folks came up from Rhode Island. I used to work in Providence as a courier for a jewelry store a while ago. A nice man, Garrett Hunter. Maybe you've heard of him?" Richie answered.

"Yes, as a matter of fact, I met Mr. Hunter earlier this week. You say you were a courier for him. What exactly does a courier do for a jewelry store anyway?"

"I made trips to New York for him to pick up some jewelry at a wholesale house. It wasn't steady work though, so I moved to Portland for steadier work."

In the meantime, Gloria had entered the cabin, removed her hat and coat, and began loading the potbelly stove with kindling as she opened the flue. Sydney was in the bedroom unpacking some of her clothes, and heard the noise from the living room. She popped her head out of the door, and faced Gloria's back.

"Oh, hi, I'm Sydney, who are you?" she asked with a smile on her face.

Gloria, by instinct, turned to greet Sydney in an unsuspecting way. As they looked at each other, they froze. Both of them were speechless. Then Sydney burst out.

"Oh, my God, Gloria, it's you, it's really you."

They hugged each other tightly for minutes as both

of them cried uncontrollably. It was a moment they both knew would happen one day.

"I am so sorry for everything, Syd. I didn't think I'd ever see you again."

"Sorry, sorry for what? Sorry for not answering my letters all those years, okay. Sorry for just cutting off your best friend in the whole world nearly twenty years ago, okay. But why, Gloria, why?"

"Because my father…" she began.

"Stop it. Stop it right now. Your father has lived with the accident all these years, and I don't blame him, Gloria, I never did. All these years you've been blaming yourself for what happened because it was your father who happened to pull the trigger. You left me in the cold all by myself when I needed you most. Not a word from you in all this time. Did your mother tell you how I went to see her just a few weeks ago? She told me you were living in Portland, and she was going to mail me your address there. Were you going to ignore my letters again?" Sydney said as her anger turned to disappointment.

"Your mom also told me about you losing your husband in Afghanistan nearly yen years ago. I lost my husband in Afghanistan, too, back in 2009. I'm just now finally seeing someone again. I hope there's a special someone in your life too. We only come this way once, Gloria, and I've wasted enough years in my life, and so have you," she went on as tears began to run down her cheek again.

"Oh, Syd, how I've missed you. You look great by the way. And this Drew Diamond who owns this place, he's the special guy you're talking about?"

"I sure hope so, because he's the best thing that's happened to me in ten years."

"I never was a person to date much to begin with, but after you and your mother left Clarksville back then, I met my husband in high school, and we got married when I was only eighteen years old. He joined the Marines in 2009, and we moved to Georgia when he was deployed to Afghanistan. He was killed just two weeks later by a sniper when his military vehicle was being used to remove landmines. After that, I went back to Portland. I still wasn't talking to my dad, so I didn't want to come back to Clarksville. I've since realized how painful I've made it for him all these years, and we're much closer again. And I met this guy, Richie, he's outside now, working with my dad. He treats me like a queen. Imagine anyone treating me like that, Syd. He's only the second man who's ever treated me that way."

"Obviously, this Richie fellow has his eyes on you. I'd like to meet him," Sydney said with a beam on her face, befitting someone who had just found a long lost friend.

When they left the cabin, they could see Richie splitting wood nearby, while Ralph was turning on the propane tank, and filling the generator with gas.

"Hello, Sydney. It's nice to see you again. I'll be inside getting the fireplace going," Ralph said, witnessing her standing close to Gloria, like a photo from years ago.

"I started the potbelly stove, Dad. And I'm pretty much done dusting and vacuuming," Gloria said.

"I'm so glad the two of you got to see each other again. It's been far too long."

"Richie, this is my childhood friend Sydney Fletcher. Oh, what did you say your married name was?"

"I didn't, but it was Malone. It's now Sydney Malone," she answered.

"You're kidding me, right? By luck, you bumped into an old friend who just happens to be staying at this cabin? And she lives in Rhode Island, too, I bet?"

"Yes, I do. I live in Cumberland."

"Mr. Diamond, over there, he knows my former boss, Garret Hunter of Hunter Jewelry in Providence. He said he talked to him just a few days ago. What a small world we live in, isn't it?"

"It sure is. What kind of work did you do for Hunter Jewelry?"

"I was a courier. I bought and sold stuff in New York for Mr. Hunter, a real nice man."

Once their chores were done, Gloria could see that her father looked exhausted. All she could imagine was him trying to do all of this work by himself. It was time for him to get back home and rest. Gloria pleaded with Sydney to stop in on Sunday before she and Drew drove back home. Sydney promised they would, but only in exchange for their phone numbers and addresses at that time.

"By the way, Syd, please tell your mom I said hi," Gloria added.

"That will be difficult. She passed away last year. She never recuperated from the accident, and that led to other ailments."

Gloria broke down and sobbed as she and Sydney hugged again, both of them in tears.

By six o'clock, Drew was getting hungry, and they left for an early dinner in Pittsburg. At the table, Drew began to talk about the coincidence of meeting Richie, who just happened to have recently worked for Hunter Jewelry.

"Imagine how many coincidences there are in this world. Who would ever think I'd meet a former employee of a guy who was very instrumental in us recovering those pearls. That's a coincidence if I've ever seen one. And although we may never catch this burglar, that's not my job, imagine the burglar being a woman with a dog bite, a tattoo on her neck, and driving an SUV with tinted windshields."

"Congratulations, Sam Spade. You've certainly made your company happy, and I'm sure that the owner of the pearls will be happy, too," she replied toasting her cocktail glass to Drew's.

"That reminds me," he added, "I've got to stop in at Hunter Jewelry on Monday to have him fill out some papers for the reward. I'll call the store and leave a message for him when we get back to the cabin."

"Did you order the carpet for the condo?" she asked.

"To be installed Monday afternoon. I move in on Tuesday," he replied.

"So does this mean we'll probably have another celebration next week?"

"Well, of course. And if you're available for about an hour on Monday, I'd like to buy a gift for my real estate agent."

"For a gift, I can be available."

When they returned to the cabin, Drew perked up

the stove and the fireplace, and excused himself for a minute as he stepped out on the front porch to make a phone call. Sydney had things to do in the bedroom.

"Mr. Hunter, this is Drew Diamond from Assurance. I have your merchandise, as I promised, and I will bring that to you on Monday. We should have no further business after that. I should be there around ten."

CHAPTER 21

THE THREAT

"Meet me outside the Providence Public Library tomor-row morning around ten. I want to buy you a gift to start your week. I have to make a quick stop in Providence on Monday morning, but you can be back at your office in Smithfield by noon," Drew told Sydney on their drive home from New Hampshire.

"Why do you want to buy me a gift?"

"Because I don't think you've received too many over the years, and it's time you did, not that I need a reason though."

As Drew stood outside the library at ten sharp on Monday, he waved to Sydney as she crossed the street from the hotel parking garage, the same place she had used several times before as a blonde. Ironically, she wore the same outfit today as she had worn on her first visit to Hunter Jewelry several weeks before, except without the blonde wig.

"The store I want to take you to is just down the street," he said with a smile as he greeted her warmly. When they reached the Hunter Jewelry storefront, Sydney paused for a moment before they entered.

"Are you okay? Is there something wrong? You look like you've just seen a ghost."

"You're taking me to a jewelry store? No one since my late husband has ever taken me to a jewelry store."

They entered the store and Garrett Hunter immediately spotted Drew as he walked to the counter and handed him a manila envelope.

"I believe you were expecting this," Drew said as he faced Garrett.

Sydney was standing behind Drew as he quickly turned to introduce her.

"We are interested in looking at some necklaces," he said.

"Certainly, Mr. Diamond, please follow me to the next counter." He glanced at Sydney and smiled.

"Have we met before? You look very familiar."

"Not at this place, I've never been in here before," she replied in a very defensive tone. "Maybe at a social function or a business meeting somewhere else."

"Would you be interested in a plain gold or silver necklace, or perhaps a string of pearls?" he asked.

"I already have a pearl necklace, thank you."

Throughout the next ten minutes, Garrett could not help but ponder where he had seen Sydney before, as she and Drew turned their attention to the various charms on display in another showcase nearby.

"Oh, what a lovely pearl bracelet this is. That would go nicely with my pearl necklace. But I bet this bracelet costs more than my costume necklace does. I don't know much about the value of pearls."

"Nonsense, Sydney. Try the bracelet on. This is my treat, something to look at when you want to think of me, or would you prefer an eight by ten photo of me for your desk at the office?" Drew replied in a playful manner as he attempted to end this whirlwind experience with the pearls. It was no wonder that Garrett sensed something about Sydney, a déjà vu moment if you will.

Then it struck Garrett like a lightning bolt. The blonde with the infamous and subsequently troublesome string of pearls, but without the blonde wig.

"Those pearls look quite nice on your wrist, madam. You seem to be a natural wearing pearls, not everyone is, you know," he mentioned in a questionable manner.

At that moment, another customer entered the store wearing a black leather coat, and stood at a different counter waiting to be served. Sydney and Drew merely glanced his way, but Garrett certainly took notice.

"Oh, by the way, Mr. Hunter, we met someone who worked for you while we were in New Hampshire this past weekend...a Richie Lamb. He said he was a courier for you on trips to New York up until a few months ago."

"I can't say who that is, Mr. Diamond. I don't know a Richie Lamb. He must have me confused with someone else. There's a Hunter Insurance Agency on Weybosset Street," Garrett answered quietly, trying not to be overheard.

"No, this guy said he used to buy and sell stuff for you, but the work wasn't steady enough, so he got a full-time job somewhere up there. He seemed like a nice hard-working guy."

Garrett took the bracelet and placed it in a gift box, and Drew paid with a credit card. They headed for the exit, and Garrett had some parting words for them.

"It was nice to see you again. Enjoy the bracelet."

Within seconds, the man in the leather jacket approached Garrett.

"My name is Tony Ferrucci. I'm taking over for Richie Volpe, and I believe you owe us quite a bit of money since the last time Richie was around."

As Garrett reached for an envelope under the counter and handed it to Ferrucci, he stated sarcastically, "And I thought you had forgotten about me."

*   *   *

Tony Ferrucci had worked for Bruno Gambardella for nearly ten years. He was an inducted member of the Santucci Family of mobsters in the Providence area, and Bruno's right hand man. Richie Volpe had, on occasion, done collections work for Ferrucci, but Richie himself had not been invited to become a life member of the crime family. After he announced his desire to quit working for Bruno, Richie was now considered an outcast. Bruno was very suspicious of Richie's intent, given the knowledge he had of the illegal businesses the family ran. Bruno's efforts to locate Richie and eliminate him became more intense as the day arrived when Bruno officially took over for Raymond Santucci. Santucci would remain as the head of the family, a position he would hold until his death, but Bruno would become the underboss in charge of all matters. Tony would become one of Bruno's capos, a promotion he long had hoped for.

"Tony, I'm asking you to take care of a loose end that's been bothering me for several months. I really think Richie knows too much, at least a lot more than he says he knows. That's a loose end that could get me in prison someday, and that bothers me. I don't want loose ends, Tony. Can I count on you to take care of this?"

"You know, Boss, I really hadn't thought much about Richie since he left. But this morning, I heard a customer at Hunter Jewelry, one of my stops, and he was talking about a Richie something or other who was a courier for Hunter, and lived in New Hampshire. How many Richie's are there out there? And what are the chances of a Richie working for one of our collection spots?"

"I don't care how you do it, Tony, just get rid of the problem for me."

"Consider it done, Boss. I'll let you know when it's over."

* * *

In the meantime, Claude Trout had left a message on Richie's cell phone informing him of the Gambardella visit to his home, and the threats of harm to his children if Trout had lied to Gambardella about not knowing Richie's whereabouts.

Richie was concerned that, through strong-arm tactics by the mob, they would somehow trace his location, especially with his mother still using her real name, Rona Volpe. A second call on his cell phone was a message from Garrett Hunter, where Garrett had mentioned the visit to his store by Drew Diamond and a female friend, who indicated they had met Richard Lamb in New Hampshire. Garrett was concerned that this conversation was overheard by Tony Ferrucci, the new collections guy now doing Richie's weekly run.

Richie wasn't sure if he should remain in Portland or not. *Will it just be a matter of time before they find me?* He pondered. For now, he chose not to worry his mother about this recent turn of events.

"Garrett, this morning you had a couple in here when I came in, and they talked about a Richie who worked for you," said Ferrucci as he approached Garrett in his store.

"The only Richie I know is the guy who took my money every week before you showed up. And he sure as hell never worked for me," Garrett answered. He didn't like Ferrucci, and he didn't hide it from him.

"Whatever happened to Richie anyway?"

"He's doing another territory these days. But you haven't seen him around, have you?"

"The last time I saw him was when he picked up his Monday morning envelope, maybe two months ago."

"Who were you talking to this morning about a Richie guy from New Hampshire?"

"His name is Drew Diamond, an insurance investigator from Assurance Property and Casualty in Lincoln. Why do you ask?"

Without answering, Tony left the store. A short trip to Assurance was in order. He arrived at Drew's office at three in the afternoon and asked to see him. When asked by the receptionist who was calling, Tony simply replied, "Tell him it's a friend of Richie from New Hampshire. He'll know who I am."

Drew was quite surprised when the receptionist left that message with his secretary.

"What do you want me to do with this," his secretary asked.

"I barely know this Richie. I met him at the cabin over the weekend. He's a friend of Miss Malone's childhood girlfriend. He was helping cut some wood for the fireplace and stove. Have this person leave a card or something at the front desk, and I'll try to reach him or her later. I don't have time for this right now. I've got to be in the general counsel's office in ten minutes.

Drew then grabbed the Conway file and headed for Bill Hart's office. The news that the pearls had been recovered, and that the insurance company did not even have to dish out the $10,000 reward for information in the case, pleased but dumbfounded Hart.

"Did the police catch the person who stole these? How did you get them back?"

"Hard to believe, Bill, but I received the stolen pearls by mail three or four days ago. No note, no reward request, nothing. Obviously, Mrs. Conway will be happy to hear the news. There were no prints on the envelope, and no way to determine who they were from. My guess is, when the person found out how much they were worth, they must have thought they were in over their heads on this."

"Well, maybe your flyers to the jewelry stores shook up somebody trying to fence them, and a jeweler convinced the fence to give them up to him, so he could return them. Do you need to do anything more on this, or can we close the file on this claim?"

"All I've got left to do is call Detective Mullen and let him know what happened. What he does is police business, and doesn't concern us."

The days were beginning to get longer, and in April, the sun was setting closer to six o'clock. When Drew left the office around five-thirty, he walked to his car in the parking lot.

"Mr. Diamond? Sorry to be bothering you, but I'm trying to get the whereabouts of Richie, you know, the guy you met in New Hampshire last weekend."

"Are you the guy who asked to see me this afternoon? Who are you?"

"Who I am is of no importance. But I need to be in touch with Richie, and Garrett Hunter told me earlier today that you had mentioned meeting a guy named Richie, who claimed to have worked for Mr. Hunter in the past. Actually, Mr. Diamond, Richie worked for my company, and we haven't seen him in months. We owe him some money."

"And what company is that, Mr.—? I didn't catch your name."

"My name and my company are not the issue here. The issue is finding where we can locate Richie Volpe."

"Perhaps I should explain to you, whatever your name is, that I am a retired police detective who doesn't take lightly to someone trying to hustle information from me, and who doesn't seem to represent a legitimate company, and doesn't want to tell me his name."

"No, Mr. Diamond, you have it all wrong. I am Anthony Ferrucci, and I work for Ocean State Olive Oil Company in Providence. I'm sorry for sounding so rude in my request. If you simply tell me where you met Richie, I'll be on my way."

"What are the odds, Mr. Ferrucci, that when I call my friends in the Providence Police Department, they tell me what the Ocean State Olive Oil Company really is, and more importantly, who you really are?"

"You're making a serious mistake, Diamond. You don't want to be on the wrong side of this conversation, if I were you."

Taking this as a threat, Drew lunged at Ferrucci, pinning him to his car with both arms in a choke hold.

"Listen, you little worm, you wait for me near my car, throw out a bullshit story about some guy I don't know, because you heard it from a weasel whom you've probably scared half to death. Who do you think you're dealing with here?"

At that moment, two security guards in the lobby of the headquarters watched the fracas through the glass windows facing the parking lot. They rushed to his aid.

"Mr. Diamond, are you okay?" one of the guards yelled.

"Yes, I'm fine, Eddie. This gentleman was just leaving."

"Goodbye, Mr. Diamond. Perhaps you and your lady friend will hear from us again soon."

Drew was agitated at this confrontation, but he tried to compose himself as he drove out of the parking lot and headed for 44 Tiffany Lane in Attleboro. He had good news for Joyce Conway, and the manila envelope on his passenger seat contained the good news. At six o'clock, he was welcomed by the Conways.

"Hi, folks. Just when you think there is no hope for recovery of stolen items, along comes a lead in the burglary, and before you know it, there is a happy ending."

Drew opened the manila envelope and handed Joyce the string of pearls and the matching ring. Her eyes lit up in excitement at the site of her heirloom.

"Oh, Ray, they got my pearls back," she uttered in disbelief as she began to cry. She held the pearls to her face, and placed the ring on one of her fingers as she held them like a person holds a long lost friend. She had not realized until then just how much the pearl necklace and ring meant to her.

"These are going in the safe from now on. I don't ever want to have to worry about some intruder doing this again. Thank you so much, Mr. Diamond. It's never been about the insurance money. It's the only remembrance of my grandmother and grandfather. I wish I had known them better."

Joyce kissed Drew on the cheek and Ray shook his hand in deep gratitude. As Drew left the house, he smiled broadly in satisfaction at what had just occurred. Joyce, on the other hand, walked quietly to the bedroom and gazed at her grandparents' photo on her dresser. She picked up the black and white photo and touched it gently.

"Ray, maybe it's time for us to think about a trip to Margarita Island. I think we're overdue to visit their gravesite. And while we're there, we should visit my mom's grave, too. We should have done it long ago."

She once again held the strand of pearls against her heart, and closed her eyes for ever so long.

CHAPTER 22

FIRST DATE

Richie was very nervous. His mother had told him to in-
vite Gloria to dinner on Thursday night. She wanted to
meet her and knew that Richie wouldn't ask his mother to go out of her way to prepare dinner for company.
The truth was, Rona was going stir crazy cooped up in
the apartment most days. The smell of spring in the air in
April once again made her want to become more active,
and return to work soon.

Surgery on one of her bad knees was scheduled for
mid-June, and the prognosis for full usage was expected
to be in late August, following extensive rehabilitation
several times a week. Although Richie had suggested to
his mother that she postpone the dinner invitation until
the therapy was done, she wanted to meet this woman
whom her son couldn't stop talking about. She had never
seen him this way, a love-stricken man for the first time.

"Gloria," he said to her on Tuesday morning as he stood at the counter about to order breakfast, "my mom wants to meet you, and has invited you to dinner at our place on Thursday. She said she wouldn't take no for an answer, and asked if there was anything you didn't eat?"

"So, she wants to check me out, does she? Wants to know who this Gloria is you keep talking about. This is more attention than I've received in a long long time, Richie. But if it will make your mother happy, sure I'll come, but I don't eat red meat of any kind. Chicken or turkey, and seafood, are fine. I like my white meat moist, the seafood steamed or broiled, not fried, with just a bit of salt. I only eat wheat or dark bread, too."

"You do not! You had fried clams in New Hampshire, and then fried chicken on Sunday afternoon before we came back."

`"Okay, so I did. I'm only kidding, but I really don't eat any red meat or pork. Anything else is fine. Tell her I'll be happy to go to dinner at your house, but only if I can bring dessert once I know what she is serving."

"Shall I pick you up around five-thirty?" he asked.

"Don't be silly. I'll drive over myself. Just let me know tomorrow what we're having, so I have the proper dessert."

Thursday came fast. Rona would prepare an egg-plant casserole with penne and marinara sauce, with a side of turkey meatballs and warm rolls. They would start the meal with a small garden salad while the casserole was still in the oven. That would give Rona ample time to get to know Gloria before serving the main course. Richie was in charge of the wine selection and had two bottles

of DaVinci Chianti on hand. Upon learning of the total-
ly Italian menu, Gloria told Richie the dessert would be
her personally prepared version of tiramisu. When she
arrived, she knocked on the front door of the first floor
apartment precisely at five-thirty.

"Welcome to my Italian castle," he said with a grin on
his face. He took the covered platter from her hands, and
placed it on the coffee table as he then offered to take
her coat.

Rona heard the conversation and slowly limped her
way into the living room to greet Gloria.

"So, this is Gloria, the woman who my son always talks
about. I am so happy to meet you, my dear. We will chat
more at dinner, but for now, I am needed in the kitchen."

"Can I help? Please, I can do the salad, or whatever."

"No, that is not necessary, I have everything under
control. You can help when I'm ready to serve, in about
thirty minutes. The casserole is in the oven, and the salad
and meatballs, turkey of course, will be ready soon. Enjoy
a nice glass of wine with Richie in the living room."

As Richie and Gloria sat next to each other on the
sofa and clanged glasses in the gesture of a toast, Rona
smiled at the sight of her son acting like a perfect gentleman. Gloria did not appear to be well off based on her
clothing, but she could tell that Richie looked past all of
that at someone who really cared for him. He was a rug-
ged man, easily capable of doing heavy physical work, his
face reminiscent of a character like Sylvester Stallone in
Rocky, or Arnold Schwarzenegger's *Terminator* role.

Rona thought, *this woman makes my son smile, and she*

sees in him what I have always seen, a tough guy with a heart of gold, who wouldn't hurt anyone unless that someone forced him to do so. They both have had difficult upbringings in their teens, and both believe that there now might be a future filled without the tough memories of their earlier years.

Dinner was perfect. The casserole and meatballs were delicious, and Gloria's tiramisu was a fitting ending to the meal. Rona and Gloria both loved cooking, and that's all they needed to know about each other. Rona could easily see why Richie was attracted to this woman, and the evening continued until nearly nine o'clock, when Gloria had to leave. Her morning at the college cafeteria meant she had to get up around five in the morning. She insisted they keep the rest of the dessert, and thanked Rona sincerely with a kiss on the cheek and a hug. The two really hit it off.

Standing at the doorway, as Richie helped her with her hat and coat, he leaned forward and kissed her for the first time. Both of them realized at that moment that this was just the beginning of something special.

* * *

Meanwhile, Drew was taking Tuesday through Friday off from work to handle the move into his new condo. He had been busily packing up dishes, food, clothing, everything he could easily transport to the condo from his apartment. The condo was only a few miles away, and he planned on making several trips there before the movers arrived to transport his furniture and other heavy items. Sydney would be there late in the afternoon on Tuesday to help with the kitchen setup, while Drew took care of rehanging his clothes at the condo. By five o'clock, the place started to look like something. The smell of new carpets and painted walls added to the newness of the condo, sort of like a new car scent does.

"So, what do you think? This place is much nicer than when I came to see it just about a month ago."

"In the tradition of Drew Diamond, this calls for a celebration," Sydney proclaimed as she opened a small cooler she had brought with her that afternoon, and popped open a small bottle of Brut and poured it into two chilled stemmed champagne glasses.

Drew laughed as he kissed her warmly for the gesture.

"Let's take a break. There's room on these two stools on the island," he said.

"Do you remember your friend Gloria's male friend from Portland, who was helping her father last week up at the cabin?' he began.

"Yes, of course. His name was Richie something or other."

"Richie Lamb. I remember it like it was yesterday."

"Why do you bring him up now?" she asked with a puzzled look.

"I had a guy come to my office yesterday wanting to know where he could find him in New Hampshire. But he called him Richie Volpe. This guy was Anthony Ferrucci, not a nice man."

"What did he want with Richie, whatever his last name was?" she asked.

"Some bullshit story about owing him money. Who

pursues a person they owe money to, even threatening them if they don't cooperate?"

"Did he threaten you?"

"He said I'd be sorry by not telling him what he wanted to hear. He even suggested that the two of us should watch out for any future visits from him. That sounded like a threat to me, and I don't take lightly to threats. So I called my friend at the Providence Police Department, and asked him about both Richie Volpe and Anthony Ferrucci. I asked him, when he had the chance, to find out who they were. He told me he didn't need time to look them up."

"What do you mean?"

"Both of them are part of the Santucci mob family in Providence, and Ferrucci is one of the top lieutenants for Bruno Gambardella, the number two guy in the mob, and soon to take it over from Santucci. I wonder if Gloria knows who she is dealing with."

"Oh, dear, he seemed like such a nice guy. This isn't something I can just call her up about. We're just finally getting back together, and this is very sensitive."

"I was thinking the same thing. I don't have a clue how to contact this Richie guy. Gloria is the only one who knows that. We need to find a subtle way to talk to Gloria first, and get Richie's whereabouts from her. How do we do that without her wondering why we're asking about her guy?"

"Look, you've got the rest of the week off from work, right? Suppose I call her and tell her you have some business in Portland on Friday, and I'm coming up, too, to keep you company on the drive. And maybe we can go to an early dinner up there with her and Richie. She'll probably call me back after she talks to him. I can go to where she works during the day while you're attending your meeting. Once I find out where he works, you can pay him a visit."

"You know what I like about you, Sydney Malone, you think, and you care deeply about people close to you, something you haven't had much of in the last few years. Somehow, I know you would be there for me, if I needed you."

"In a heartbeat, Diamond, I'm more sure of it every day that goes by.'

They kissed once, then again, and suddenly the champagne toast was irrelevant. The distraction lasted for nearly an hour or so. Then Sydney called Gloria to make the arrangements. Within minutes, she returned to the kitchen and faced Drew.

"What time do we leave on Friday morning? She works at the University of Southern Maine in Portland in the students' dining hall until two. I told her I'd meet her there at lunchtime."

"I'll pick you up at eight. That should get us there way before noon. As soon as you find out where Richie works, find a reason to excuse yourself so you can make a call to me. Then I'll pick you up around two o'clock or so."

"Now, where were we before this interruption?" she asked.

CHAPTER 23

THE CONFRONTATION

Friday morning came fast, as Drew had spent the rest of his time off opening and unpacking boxes, hanging up artwork on the walls, coordinating the connection for his phone service and cable connection, and getting used to the neighborhood and the noise, mostly the lack of noise. The peace and quiet from the abutting neighbor was refreshing, partly due to the triple-insulated walls between them, but also because the neighbor travelled on business often, leaving an empty condo next door.

Drew was worried about the impending conversation he was about to have with Richie Lamb, according to Gloria, but Richie Volpe if you listened to Tony Ferrucci. For Sydney's sake, he didn't want to suddenly disrupt the newfound bond between childhood friends, but he didn't know what to expect from the confrontation. Sydney was worried for Gloria, and how she would react to finding out that Richie had an affiliation with the Rhode Island mafia. The ride to Portland was unusually quiet.

Sydney went over her approach to Gloria in her mind, very mindful of not arousing any suspicion from her as a result of their casual conversation. Drew, on the other hand, had no problem in being very direct with Richie. His former lengthy stint as a Worcester police detective would make his meeting reminiscent of his police interrogation days not so long ago. Even at age fifty-six, he had his ways of handling criminals of all sorts.

Three hours later, they arrived in Portland, an hour before Sydney's noon meeting with Gloria. They killed time by retrieving information off their smartphones, and by eleven forty-five, they drove toward the dining hall parking lot for visitors.

"Call me the minute you find out where he works," he told her. "Be very calm with her. There's no need yet to alarm her about this guy. Let me talk to him first."

Sydney walked into the building and proceeded toward the lunch line in the cafeteria. She spotted Gloria taking lunch orders from students as she worked diligently in this rapid paced environment. Students often had little time to spend between classes. She watched as Gloria was calm and very proficient at what she did. The students liked her, Sydney could tell as they often smiled, and thanked her for the attention she gave to each of them.

"Can I help you?" Gloria asked, not so much as looking up to see who the next person in line was.

"I am beyond help, Miss, but perhaps you can save me."

"Syd, great that you could make it. Can you give me about fifteen minutes to take care of all these people? They kind of eat on the fly, and I'm the one who can keep them on schedule."

"No problem. I'll grab a sandwich and a Coke, and I'll be over in that corner at one of the tables."

Twenty minutes later, the lunch line had slowed down to a crawl, and Gloria made her way to Sydney's table after asking her assistant to handle any new orders.

"Drew has an insurance meeting with another investigator here in Portland, and he won't be out of that meeting until after two. I thought we could chat for a little while during your lunch break. You do have a lunch break, I hope."

"Only thirty minutes, because I get off at two. Richie gets off at three, so we can have an early dinner at a nearby restaurant, say around four o'clock, and you guys can be on your way back by six. You'll probably get back to Rhode Island around nine. There won't be any traffic at this time of year, weekend or no weekend."

"What does Richie do for a living? Most people get off at five or six. I bet it's construction if he finishes at three?" Sydney asked.

"No, he works on campus for the athletic department. He's one of the maintenance workers. He mows the lawns on the athletic fields, works on gyms and auditorium floors, all that kind of stuff. They really like him. He's a hard worker, and minds his own business."

"I think I drank that Coke too fast. Can you point me to the ladies room? I'll be right back."

"Sure. Just go out those doors and take a left. The bathrooms will be on your right just a few feet away."

She entered the bathroom, went into a stall, and closed the door. She pulled out her smartphone and called Drew with the information.

"Wish me luck. I have no idea how this will work out."

Sydney walked back to her table and smiled at Gloria.

"This Richie seems to be a nice man, Gloria."

"He sure is. He treats me like a queen. He takes care of his mother, a very sweet person, and just wants to make something of his life. I can relate to that. It's been a tough ten years since Jesse died. And there was nothing for me back in Clarksville."

"What do you know about him? I mean, where does he come from?"

"He's from where you are now, Rhode Island. He couldn't find steady work there, and he needs a good job to take care of his mother. She needs knee surgery, and his last job didn't have any medical coverage. So he came up here, hoping to find something, and he did. I think he'll do well up here."

Meanwhile, Drew drove toward the athletic complex on the lower end of the campus. He entered the office at the front of the gymnasium, and asked to see Richard Lamb, a maintenance worker.

"I'm a friend of his from Rhode Island, and I was hoping I could just say hi."

Jenny, the athletic department secretary, liked Richie, and thought Drew was genuine in his request. She picked up the phone, called the maintenance number, and asked where Richie was working that day.

"You can find him in the football stadium mowing the grass. Take your next right, and you'll see the stadium about two hundred yards ahead."

He parked his car in front of the main entrance to the stadium, and walked through the concession area toward the field. He walked up the entry ramp to the stands and could see Richie on a riding mower at the far end near the goal posts. Drew jumped the railing onto the playing field and began the walk toward Richie.

Richie noticed someone walking his way and, after he raised his mower blades, began to drive the mower toward the person approaching. Suddenly, he stopped, noticing that it was Drew, and got off the mower, turning off the engine.

"Mr. Diamond? What are you doing here? I didn't expect to see you until later this afternoon. Gloria said we were meeting for an early dinner somewhere."

"Actually, Richie, I needed to talk to you before dinner. Is there a better place than right here to talk?" Drew asked as there was no one else visible in the whole stadium.

"No, this is fine, unless you'd rather sit down in the stands over there," Richie pointed to some box seats nearby. "What's this about, sir?"

"Maybe that would be better," he answered as they both sat down.

"Two days ago, I got a visitor in the parking lot at the insurance company I work for in Lincoln. The guy's name was Tony Ferrucci. He had been told by Garrett Hunter that maybe I knew where Richie Volpe was. Sydney and I happened to be in his store last week and I mentioned that I met you in New Hampshire and you had worked for him. He said he didn't know a Richie Lamb, and you most certainly never worked for him. Before I became an insurance investigator, I was a cop for nearly thirty-five years in Worcester. When I called my old friend at the Providence Police Department, you probably know what he told me about Tony Ferrucci and Richie Volpe."

Richie showed no surprise on his face. He knew that one day Bruno Gambardella would track him down. He hadn't expected it to be this soon.

"Mr. Diamond, I have been a collection man for Gambardella since I was a teenager. My mother wanted me off the streets in Providence while she worked two jobs to support us, and Gambardella convinced my mother that he could teach me good business things when I got out of school each afternoon. I'm thirty-two, and I was still collecting money for him, going absolutely nowhere with my life, and I didn't want to do it anymore," he began.

"So, a couple of months ago, I told him I wanted to take my mother to a warmer climate because of her bad knees, where they wouldn't hurt as much until I could get her replacements for the bum knees. I sensed that he thought I knew too much about the family business, but he agreed to let me go when I told him all I knew was my collection territory, period. When I was packing up to move, he sent two of his goons to my mother's apartment, but I managed to get away before they saw me. I may not be the brightest bulb on the planet, Mr. Diamond, but I knew they weren't planning a social visit," he went on.

"I picked up my mother and never looked back. But rather than go south as I told him, we came up here to Portland, and I changed my name to Richard Lamb. I got the maintenance job here a few months ago, and my mother and I are doing okay. Because of the medical coverage I have, she's going to have surgery this summer for one of the knees. I met Gloria in the cafeteria one morning, and I really like her, Mr. Diamond. She's the first woman who thinks I'm wonderful, and I think the same about her. Does she need to know what I did before I came up here? I never hurt anyone, and I'm not a member of the family. But to Bruno, as nice as he's been to my mother and me, I'm not needed anymore. I know what that means, Mr. Diamond. That's why Ferrucci's looking for me. I don't fit into the witness protection program, because I haven't testified against anyone."

"You know that Sydney has been looking forward to reuniting with Gloria for many, many years. If she spoke badly about you to her, she might never get another chance to get close to her again. But, here's the deal. You decide whether you're going to tell her about your past. I don't care if you tell her this weekend, next year, or even never, if that's what you decide. And if you decide to tell her, you're never to mention that I know, or that Sydney knows who you were. Is that clear?"

"You're only the third person I've ever met that gave me a break. Believe it or not, Garrett Hunter was the first one to tell me to get out while I could. Then the recruiter for the college up here gave me a break with the job, even though I had no experience. And now you, Mr. Diamond. Why are you keeping this quiet?"

"I told you, I don't want Sydney to lose a friend because of this. She doesn't have any other childhood friends that I've heard of. But that's not the only reason. If you really want out from these guys, you've almost got to disappear, not exist anymore. Without witness protection, they might find you. Portland's a popular place, and someone might see you one day. Even ten years from now, they don't forget you're still out there. You've got to be either dead or someplace they'll never find you. Maybe I can figure something out. In the meantime, if I were you, I'd socialize in small restaurants most of the time just to be safe. And I'd definitely change my appearance to disguise my face a bit, add a pair of glasses, grow a beard, or shave my head, something to make myself look different. Sydney and I will see you later today for a quick bite. This conversation never happened."

By two-thirty, Drew entered the cafeteria and saw Sydney sitting at a table fumbling through her smartphone. When she saw him approaching, she didn't know whether to smile or be nervous at what he had to say.

"Well, how did it go?" she asked doubtfully.

"It went well. He's the same guy, but he's changed his name to get away from that kind of life. I tend to believe him. How many hoods would give up their affiliation with the mob to mow the lawn at a football stadium? He thinks they want him dead because they're afraid he knows too much about their crooked operations. He's right. If they find Richie Volpe, he's as good as dead. I'll talk to some guys in Providence on Monday, and see if they have any advice."

"So, we're still on for dinner at four with them?" Drew asked.

"As far as I know. Gloria just left, and we're supposed to meet them at the Piccolo Restaurant on Middle Street by then."

Drew had not noticed the black Chevy Impala that had followed them at a distance all the way to Portland. Tony Ferrucci had decided to follow the couple as soon as he saw Drew pick up Sydney that morning.

Traffic was heavy, as weekenders, travelling to the lakes of New Hampshire and Maine, or to the seaside, would get a head start by leaving on Friday morning. Although traffic was certainly not as heavy as during the summer months, April was the month that people owning a vacation home used to re-open their vacation properties dormant over the winter months.

A single idle threat in the parking lot at Assurance was not reason enough for Drew to keep a furtive eye on cars seemingly following him that day. But as he and Sydney walked out of the campus dining hall, Drew made note of a black sedan, with Rhode Island license plates, parked a short distance from his vehicle in the parking lot. He could not make out the figure inside the sedan as the front windshield was heavily tinted. As they walked past the black car, the driver side window also was tinted, and the motor was running.

"Call Gloria. Tell her we'll meet them inside the restaurant at four, but if we're a few minutes late, tell her to order us two martinis, and to find a quiet spot in a dark corner of the place. If she asks why, tell her I've got an eye infection, and too much lighting hurts my eyes."

"What's going on? What's this all about?"

"I think we've got company, a car from Rhode Island with the motor running is right down the way in the next row of the lot."

He quickly grabbed a pad from the center console and jotted down the license plate numbers. Sydney began to get nervous. She punched in Gloria's cell phone number, and when Gloria answered, she repeated what Drew had told her to say, trying desperately to sound convincing.

Drew started the car and slowly pulled out of the parking lot, never once looking toward the black sedan nearby.

"Let's see if I'm just paranoid right now, or if there really is someone following us today. I sure hope if it is a tail, he wasn't inside the stadium when I was talking to Richie. This has to be Ferrucci or one of his men."

He drove slowly until he was off campus and then continued toward downtown Portland, all the while glancing in his rear view mirror to see if they were being followed. Sure enough, the black sedan was about five hundred feet behind them, about the fourth car trailing theirs. Drew quickly entered the Maine Mall, parked his car in front of the Villa Italian Kitchen as he and Sydney went inside. It was now two-thirty and Drew had to think fast at how he would avoid being followed for their rendezvous with Gloria and Richie at four o'clock, about two miles from the restaurant they were in. Drew walked up to the barmaid behind the counter.

"Excuse me, Miss, perhaps you can help us? My wife's ex-boyfriend appears to be stalking us today. He's in a car outside and seems to be following us everywhere. Is there a way we can take a taxi out a back door from here without being noticed?" he asked flashing a twenty dollar bill in his hand.

"Creep. Guys like that can be a royal pain. I'll call the taxi company I use, and tell them to pick you up behind the mall at my back door. He'll take you wherever you want to go. You can keep your money, Mister, I had a guy like that once, a real haunt," the barmaid said as she called for a taxi with special directions for the pickup.

"You can go out the back door through the kitchen and watch for him. He'll be here in a couple of minutes."

They thanked the woman and went into the kitchen and walked to the rear door of the restaurant at the back of the mall. Within minutes, the taxi arrived and they quickly jumped in, and told the driver the address they wanted to go to. As the taxi emerged from the rear of the mall and headed for the mall exit, Drew and Sydney laid low behind the back seat until they were beyond the mall. Ten minutes later, they arrived at Piccolo's. It was three-thirty and the restaurant lot was virtually empty. Although the dining area only opened at four, the bar area had been open since one o'clock, and they entered the lounge and sat at the bar area.

At ten minutes to four, Gloria and Richie entered and the four proceeded to enter the dining room and ordered quickly. They had idle conversation throughout the meal, Richie avoiding any eye contact with Drew for most of the time. Sydney and Gloria, on the other hand, wanted to cram ten years of events in their lives into this one dinner. It was a wonder they actually finished their meals.

At six, they said goodbye to Gloria and Richie, and asked the waiter to call a cab for them. Drew gave the waiter the cab driver's card.

"A cab, what do you need a cab for? Where's your car?" asked Richie.

"Minor skips in the motor. It'll be ready for me to pick up though. They thought it might be water in the gas line. We're fine," echoed Drew.

"We can drop you off. No need for a cab," Gloria chimed in.

"Oh no," Drew interjected. "That's part of the service from the repairman. His brother runs a taxi service like Uber, and rather than invest in a loaner vehicle, he gets the guy to take you anywhere locally. Thanks for the offer though. You guys can chat for a couple of minutes more while I go out and wait for him to get here."

"This was great, Gloria," Sydney said. "Thanks for having dinner with us. Keep in touch. I don't know when Drew is planning on going back to the cabin in Pittsburg, but I imagine he'll want to go up a few times this summer."

Drew reappeared when the taxi arrived, and he had scoured the area to make sure there was no black sedan around. The trip back to the Villa Italian Kitchen took fifteen minutes, and Drew had the taxi drop them off at the rear entrance again. They left through the front door and got in his car. At six-fifteen, it was starting to get dark outside, and Drew started the car and his headlights automatically went on. The GPS on his dashboard led him back to the Maine Turnpike and then Route 95 South.

They made one stop in Chelmsford, Massachusetts at a Dunkin' Donuts just off Route 495. Drew sat briefly with a cup of coffee as Sydney went to the ladies room. He glanced outside only to see a parked black sedan with the headlights on at the far end of the lot. He tried to ignore it, but his first glance must have frightened the driver, and the car left the parking lot. Sydney came out of the ladies room and the rest of the ride home was uneventful.

"Use the deadbolt, the chain, and the bottom locks on your apartment for now. I'm not having a good feeling about this Ferrucci guy," he said in a serious tone to Sydney. "Or you can stay at my place tonight if you want to."

"No, I'm okay. I'll call you tomorrow to put some finishing touches in the condo, if you want me to? I think I need my bed tonight. It's been a long day."

"Tomorrow would be great. Maybe after lunch sometime."

As she entered the apartment building, Drew made sure the outside door was locked after she entered. When he returned to his car, he reached into the glove box and pulled out a nine millimeter pistol, and placed it on the passenger seat nearby. He arrived at his condo five minutes later and drove into his garage at the rear of the unit without anyone in sight.

He would call Detective Mullen in the morning to get the owner's name off the license plate number.

CHAPTER 24

THE FBI

"License Plate F-324 is a black 2018 Chevrolet Impala, owned by Anthony Ferrucci, 32 Crystal Lane, Cranston," Detective Mullen told Drew on Monday morning. "Why are you messing around with a guy like that?"

"I'm not, but his car was always close to mine over the weekend, even in Maine."

"You'd better report this to the FBI, Drew. Why in the world would they be following you?"

"I have no clue, but I'm sure about the car following me around all weekend."

As he sat at his desk in his office at Assurance on Monday morning, he started scrolling his old Rolodex file for a particular name. Minutes later, there it was, under FBI, Providence Bureau, Sean Connors. The name had been inserted over the scratched out name of Harry Esten, Senior Agent. Drew remembered meeting Con-

nors and Esten at a seminar put on by the FBI for Massachusetts detectives back in 2014. He had heard of Esten's
retirement, and hoped Connors was still there.

"Sean, Drew Diamond from the Worcester Police."

"Drew, how the heck are you? I thought I read somewhere where you retired from the force," Connors answered.

"I did, about two years ago now. I'm an investigator at
Assurance Property & Casualty in Lincoln. I've got a situa-
tion that came up, and I could use your advice. It involves
Tony Ferrucci."

"Tony Ferrucci, what in the world do you have in
common with Tony Ferrucci?"

"It's a long story, and I think it involves a contract on
a guy named Richie Volpe."

"Volpe, he's nobody, just a gofer for Gambardella.
We have nothing on him as far back as stupid kids' stuff
when he was a teenager. Why would he be a target? He's
certainly not talking to us about anything."

"Can we meet for lunch? I'll treat you to lunch at
Trattoria Romana in Lincoln."

"I can do lunch. I'll bring Tom Donnelly along, he's
the bureau's expert on the Santucci Family."

At lunch, Drew related the story about his meeting
with Ferrucci in the insurance company parking lot, and
his threats to him if he didn't divulge where he had spoken to Richie Volpe in New Hampshire. He then told
them about his meeting with Volpe and Richie's plan to
walk away from the mob and disappear without the use of
witness protection.

"Nobody just walks away," Donnelly told Drew. "Any threat to their domain gets eliminated, never to be heard from again. I wish Volpe had come to us first."

"Because he truly knows very little about anything the family does, except for the collections he was responsible for, he figured he would never qualify for witness protection, because he had nothing to offer you guys. He's got a regular job, takes care of his mother, and even has a girlfriend, a very sweet girl. Is there some way he can beat this?"

"We would need to make Volpe dead. An unrecognizable death, publicized in the Providence paper where they would see it, that might do the trick. We've used this a few times over the years, in conjunction with houses blowing up from gas explosions, or a fake car crash where the bodies were just not recognizable, stuff like that. Once or twice, we've done this for some of our witnesses going into the witness protection system. It's all a matter of whether the mob believes it or not," Donnelly stated.

"I'd like to give this guy a chance to make it. He's not a bad guy, and he just doesn't know where to turn for help."

"Find out if Volpe still owns the same car he had when he was in Providence. Chances are he still does, and he might even still be driving with a Rhode Island plate. Although that's not the dumbest thing to do, it's right up there with items from your past you need to get rid of. But if he still drives the same car, maybe we can use that." Donnelly waved his hand across the front of Drew, as if reading a newspaper highlight.

Mother and son killed in head-on crash with hit and run driver. Pickup truck causes fiery crash, then flees scene. Victims identified from dental records and the license plate on their vehicle were Rona Volpe and her son Richard Volpe of Dover, New Hampshire. No other relatives have been located at this time. The pickup truck responsible has not been located and the investigation is ongoing. The victims' remains were cremated, should anyone come forth to claim them.

"You could do that? You could fake Richie's death and his mother's too?"

"If he changes his name, some of his physical appearance, and the mother does, too, it often ends it, especially if it's a small-time guy like Volpe. He's not a major witness in a mob hit, or the accountant for the Santuccis. He's just a collector. Gambardella's the new boss now that Santucci has stepped down, and he's very cautious not to be implicated in anything at this early stage of his rule. Anyone's expendable with Bruno."

"So, if he's still using the car, what do we do?" asked Drew.

"We can understand Volpe wanting to keep his new name and location secret, that's fine. If we can convince our boss that he's not living a life of crime in New Hampshire, or wherever he is, and that you will vouch for his character, I'll let you know what's next. Don't talk to Ferrucci again, even if he tries to scare you. It's important that he remains unsure of what you know about Volpe. If he had spotted Volpe in that stadium on Friday, we wouldn't be having this conversation right now, and you wouldn't have seen Ferrucci's car when you left the cafeteria with your girlfriend. He would have stayed at the stadium, focusing on Volpe, not you. So it's probably safe to say he didn't see him yet. Sean will call you with any news. In the meantime, have Volpe get that car off the road until we call. If he can buy another one with a new driver's license under his new name, tell him to do it now."

Later that afternoon, Drew reached for a cell phone number he had jotted down on the back of one of his business cards in his wallet. He called the number.

"Richie, this is Drew Diamond. Don't talk for now, just listen. I'm working on making you disappear for good. But first, you need to take your car off the road for now, and buy another one. Don't get rid of the car yet. Does it still have Rhode Island plates?"

"Yes, I haven't received my Maine license yet under Richard Lamb, so I wanted to wait to register it then."

"Rent a car, or take a bus to and from work for now. When do you expect to get the license?"

"I've got a temporary one now, but the new one should be in any day now. Why do I need to get rid of my car?"

"By dumb luck, if somebody sees you and thinks of whom you look like, seeing you in the same car you drove in Providence will be too much of a coincidence. It's not worth the risk, and besides, the FBI will need it if they agree to help."

"You told the FBI about me? Why did you do that?"

"Because they know how to make people disappear, even without going into witness protection. Don't worry, I haven't told them where you are, or what your name is, and I won't. But whatever they do, your car will likely play a role. As soon as you get your new license, buy another car, but get the one you have now off the road," Drew emphasized.

"Why would the FBI help me? I don't have anything to give them. I told you I know nothing about what goes on inside the Santucci Family, other than my collections."

"Because I asked them to. I told them I would vouch for you. I'm hoping that means something with my thirty-five years of police work. And until I tell you otherwise, start going to small restaurants when you're out with Gloria, no place where tourists usually go on vacations to Portland. They also said you need to change your appearance. Grow a beard or a mustache, and wear glasses. Think about changing your hair style, more hair or go bald, either one. You minimize the chance of anyone recognizing you that way. If you decide not to tell Gloria about your past, you'll need to convince her you've decided to make these changes on your own. Good luck with that, but start making some facial changes now, even if it's only a pair of glasses and a new hairdo. I'll get back to you as soon as I hear anything from the FBI."

The following day at nine o'clock in the morning, the doorbell rang at 32 Crystal Lane, Cranston. A woman answered.

"Can I help you?" she asked as she faced two men in suits standing at her doorway.

"Is Tony home, please? Agents Donnelly and Connors from the FBI," Donnelly politely asked as they flashed their badges at the woman.

Within minutes, Ferrucci appeared from the kitchen, still in an undershirt and a pair of dark pants.

"Gentlemen, so nice to see you. To what do I owe the pleasure?" he asked sarcastically.

"We have received a complaint from Mr. Drew Diamond that you recently made threats against him in a parking lot at Assurance Insurance in Lincoln."

"I don't believe I know the man, Agent Donnelly. And this is an item for the FBI to get involved in, not the local police?"

"There were two security guards who said they witnessed the incident, Mr. Ferrucci."

"There is no way any security guards heard any of the conversation I may have had, if I had any conversation at all with this Mr. Diamond person. But the last time I checked, a conversation with someone is not illegal, is it?"

"No, but a threat is. Mr. Diamond is a law-abiding citizen, a retired police detective, and a friend of the bureau, Mr. Ferrucci. Leave him alone, or we will be back. Is that clear?" Donnelly stressed.

"I believe we are done here, gentlemen. You both have a nice day," Ferrucci uttered with a smile on his face as he closed the door in their faces.

As Donnelly and Connors walked back to their car, Donnelly looked at Connors, and said.

"Well, that should set the stage for our next move, assuming the chief okays us to move forward."

Later that afternoon, both of them stood before the bureau chief pleading their case for helping Richie Volpe disappear. Based on the endorsement of a highly respected former police officer, and the recommendation from two FBI agents, the chief told them that no official act from the bureau could be made since there was to be no exchange of information from Volpe. The words 'no official act' stood out with Connors and Donnelly as meaning the bureau would look the other way if the agents were involved in any action that would appear to remove the name of Richie Volpe from existence. The bureau chief would deny any involvement in such action.

* * *

The ad in the *Concord Monitor* listed the four room apartment for rent in Dover, New Hampshire. An older woman and a younger man filled out the application form and presented it to the owners, a retired couple. The names on the form were Rona Volpe and Richard Volpe. Two agents, who closely resembled Rona and Richie, secured the apartment with a two-month advance rent payment.

Drew relayed to Richie to drive his car to the High-Hanover Parking Garage at 34 Hanover Street, Portsmouth, New Hampshire on Wednesday by six o'clock at night, and park the vehicle on the third level. Drew told Richie to leave the keys and the parking stub under the mat on the passenger side of the car. He was then to walk to the bus stop at 54 Hanover Street and wait for the seven o'clock Greyhound bus back to Portland. Since there was no bus terminal in Portsmouth, Richie was to buy his one-way ticket from Portsmouth to Portland at the Portland Greyhound terminal ahead of time. Once back in Portland, he was to buy another car the following day if at all possible, regardless of having received his permanent license or not. Dealers would accept his temporary one if that's all he had at the time.

Later that week, in the Saturday edition of the *Providence Journal*, under Regional News, there stood two photos, one of Rona Volpe, and the other of Richard Volpe.

Dover, NH: A mother and her adult son were killed on Thursday night as the result of a head-on crash with a pickup truck driven by a hit and run driver. The victims' car caught fire and they were trapped inside. They were identified by dental records and the license plate attached to the late model sedan. The hit and run driver is still at large and witnesses at the scene could only identify the vehicle as a green Ford 150 pickup. Dover police have asked local residents to report any sightings of a heavily damaged vehicle in the area. The victims were identified as Rona Volpe, 56, and her son Richard, 32, recently moved to Dover from Rhode Island. The investigation is still ongoing.

An insert in the article depicted the remains of the scorched vehicle with the entire front section folded like an accordion.

Once again the doorbell rang at Ferrucci's house, and once again Donnelly and Connors stood at the door.

"Mr. Ferrucci, can you tell us your whereabouts on Thursday evening?" asked Donnelly.

"Right here at home, watching TV with the wife," he answered.

"Is she home?"

"No, Alice is a very religious person, Mr. Donnelly. She's not back from church yet."

"What church would that be?"

"Why St. Mark Church on Garden Court."

"Sean, take the car, go to the church, and see if you can see Mrs. Ferrucci there. If she is, ask her what she did on Thursday night. Then call me. I'll stay here with this smart-ass until you call."

"What's going on here? What's this all about?" he asked angrily.

"Don't be a smart-ass, Ferrucci, you know damn well what this is about. First you threaten a guy who won't tell you where he talked to Richie Volpe in New Hampshire, and then you orchestrate a hit and run to make his death look like an accident after you find out where he is. This guy was a nobody. Gambardella must be paranoid. All because this Volpe wanted out of the family. You're disgusting."

"What the hell are you talking about? I didn't have Volpe killed. Where the hell did you get that idea," he asked with a puzzled look on his face.

Donnelly took the folded newspaper from under his arm and flashed the article in the morning paper in front of Ferrucci.

"I'll be damned. No way, I'm telling you, I was home on Thursday all night long. You won't hear anything different from my wife, you'll see."

Donnelly's cell phone buzzed, and he picked it up quickly. After a few seconds, he hung up.

"You haven't heard the last from us on this, you piece of trash. I know you had something to do with this, and we'll get to the bottom of this. I want to be the first to slap the cuffs on you, pal. You're nothing but a peon working for Gambardella, and he'd better watch himself carefully, because we'll take him down too."

"Back off, Donnelly. You obviously have no way to implicate me in this unfortunate tragedy of one of our former colleagues. We would be glad to care for his family, but it doesn't appear he had any family left."

Once Connors returned with the car, Donnelly stormed down the front walk, into the passenger side as the vehicle pulled away. As the car left the residential section of Cranston, a huge smile appeared on Donnelly's face.

"I think he believes today was his lucky day," he stated.

CHAPTER 25

PORTLAND, MAINE

Drew called Richie on Saturday afternoon after Sean Connors called him at home late that morning.

"Richie, you are officially dead. You were killed in a hit and run car crash in Dover, New Hampshire, where the FBI had rented an apartment under you and your mother's name. They showed the newspaper article to Ferrucci this morning, and it looks like it worked. The *Journal* even had your picture and that of your mother, too. She should change her name to Lamb like you just to make the switch permanent. According to my contacts, all you'll need to do is repay the Feds for the two months' rent they advanced for the apartment in Dover. Your old car was burnt to a crisp, and your remains and your mother's were unrecognizable."

"I can't believe this, Mr. Diamond. I really didn't want to tell Gloria about what I did before I came up here, and I'm really getting attached to this place. My mother will catch on, too, once her knees are better, and she gets out more. There's a future for me, and I will never forget what you did for me."

"Just be good to Gloria, or Sydney will be all over me if you're not."

"She is my savior. I think it's time for both of us to finally start living again. Since I met her, she makes me a better person. I can't explain it, Mr. Diamond, she's the kindest person I have ever met. Is Sydney like that too?"

"Sydney and Gloria have both had a pretty hidden life since their husbands died ten years ago. And the loss of Sydney's father from an accidental hunting accident involving Gloria's father affected Sydney's mother for the rest of her life. And it separated two childhood friends until earlier this year. You must never tell Gloria that Sydney knows about your past. If Gloria ever found out, she'd never forgive Sydney for not telling her she knew. They both don't have very many friends, neither has dated until now, and it's like they are trying to catch up on all that they've missed. I think I finally understand Sydney, and she's starting to open up a lot more."

"I think about Gloria every day, and I look forward to talking to her every day. My mother tells me she's the one. She says she knows more about Gloria than anybody, because of how much I talk about her at home. She told me to marry her before she gets away. But we've only known each other for a few months. How long have you and Sydney been together, if you don't mind my asking?"

"Probably about the same, a couple of months. She

was the real estate agent representing the former owners of the condo I just bought and moved into. I lost my
wife in a car accident two years ago, right after I retired
from the Worcester Police, so I'm no social butterfly either. She's fun to be with, she's pretty and smart, and our
age difference doesn't seem to bother her. My son's her
age, thirty-two, and he's about to get married. I'm happy
with the way things are going between us, but marriage,
that's another thing. We'll see how things work out as the
months go by."

CHAPTER 26

AUGUST,
THREE MONTHS LATER

Richie had been dating Gloria for over five months, and they had begun to talk about moving in together with Richie's mother, sharing a larger apartment, or even a five or six-room ranch house outside the metropolitan area of Portland where properties were less expensive. There no longer was any doubt in Gloria's mind that she truly loved Richie, and would cherish the day when she became Mrs. Gloria Lamb.

But Richie was still shy and nervous about asking her to marry him. Rona's surgery on her knee had gone well, and she was dedicated to speeding her rehabilitation at the Portland Therapy Center, so that she could finally go to work again. She had often told Richie that she would be fine living on her own in a small apartment, but he would not hear of it.

"I shouldn't be in the way of you young folks," she would say.

"Mom, I'm the one who's been hanging around all these years. Gloria likes you like crazy. She automatically assumes you'll be living with us, whether we're married or not," Richie would answer.

"I tried to raise you as a good Catholic boy, but you didn't make it easy, and I can see now that letting you work for Mr. Gambardella was not a good idea. You really should marry Gloria, Richie, never mind this living together for a while. Make me happy, son, ask her to marry you."

"Suppose she says no, or not now, or maybe later. Then what do I do?" he asked.

"Listen to me. I know this girl. She loves you, I can see it every time she looks at you, every time you hold a chair for her, or open a door for her. You both have had tough times, and that makes you stronger, and you're always there for each other. I would have given my right arm to have someone like that, instead of the loser I had in my life. And I see the way you look at her. It's time, Richie, it's time."

"How do I do this, Mom? I have no idea. I need a ring. How do I know what size to buy, how much to spend, all that stuff?"

"Don't worry about that stuff. If it doesn't fit, the jeweler will make it fit after you give it to her. It's not the price, it's the meaning that will sweep her off her feet. You watch, she wouldn't care if it was a cigar band you gave her. Well, maybe not a cigar band, but you know what I mean."

He wrestled with the thought of marriage, and over the next few days finally decided he would pop the question. He reached for his cell phone at lunch one day and called Garrett Hunter and left a text message.

Waldo is well, and is planning to get married. He would like to buy an engagement ring from you in the $500-$600 range, preferably a silver ring with some diamond stone in it. Can we meet Thursday at five at the usual place? Hope you are well.

Garrett never replied. Richie thought he didn't want to get involved anymore, but on a hunch that Thursday, he drove to the 110 Grill in Hopkinton, arriving shortly before five o'clock. He went inside and saw no one at the bar and turned to leave. He walked toward his car, probably unrecognizable to Garrett anyway, as he now had a full beard and wore glasses. A car with a tinted windshield pulled up nearby and Garrett got out and walked toward the restaurant.

Richie followed from a distance, sporting a baseball cap, jeans, and a Boston Red Sox t-shirt. He sat at the bar, two stools away from Garrett, and slipped him a note.

You're looking good, Garrett. Waldo

Garrett had not been looking Richie's way, but instead focused on the restaurant doorway. When he looked down momentarily, he saw the note, and began to scan the restaurant. Richie kept his head down, focused on his drink as Garrett's eyes didn't give him so much as a glance. At that moment, the bartender approached Garrett and walked past him to where Richie sat.

"Another Jack Daniel's and Coke, sir?"

"Yes, please," Richie answered.

Garrett sat there and suddenly reacted...Jack Daniel's and Coke. He looked at Richie and suddenly smiled broadly as Richie remained on his stool and looked straight ahead.

"Good God, Richie, I never would have known it was you. Things are working out for you wherever you are?" he asked.

"Getting married is usually a sign that things are going well. And you, Garrett?"

"I almost got caught getting rid of some hot stuff months ago, and I thought about my wife and kids, and what would happen to them if I wasn't there anymore. So, I took my own advice to you, I stopped doing it. I obviously don't make as much, but I sleep a lot better at night."

"Right now, Garrett, I'm the happiest man alive. I'll never be able to repay you. It's the smartest move I've made so far. Getting married may be the smartest ever. Did you bring a ring?"

Garrett reached into his pocket and pulled out a little blue felt box, and slid the box toward Richie. Richie opened it and smiled.

"If it doesn't fit right, just take it to a local jeweler, and he'll resize it for you."

Richie pulled a small envelope from his jeans, and slipped it toward Garrett.

"I think you'll find $600 in the envelope."

"As agreed," replied Garrett.

As Garrett rose to leave, he looked straight ahead,

and said to Richie.

"May you be happy in marriage, my new friend. Perhaps someday, we will meet again."

With that, he rose and headed for the exit, never turning back. Two minutes later, a waiter tapped Richie on the shoulder.

"The gentleman who just left insisted I deliver this envelope to you. You are Waldo?"

"Yes, I am," he answered.

The waiter handed Richie the same small envelope he had just given Garrett. The envelope had a note written on it.

A wedding present for the bride and groom. Be well, my friend. Garrett

As Richie began the drive back to Portland, tears flowed down his cheek. He would ask Gloria to marry him the following night.

CHAPTER 27

AFGHANISTAN 2009

Following his graduation from Pittsburg High in New Hampshire in 2007, Jesse Sokoloski was happy to be working for Timber Wolf Logging in the Northern Woods of New Hampshire. He drove a log carrier to and from White Mountain Lumber in Berlin. The pay was excellent, and the forecast for a lengthy employment looked rosy. He had met Gloria Jones during high school, and things started to get serious in their relationship as they began talking about marriage, kids, a home, and the normal stuff young lovers talk about. Gloria was not a good student in high school, and was glad she was able to become a waitress at the local diner where her mother waited on tables. Jesse and Gloria would spend weekends talking about their future plans.

However, in the summer of 2008, the lumber business took a turn for the worse, and Timber Wolf was forced to lay off many workers, including Jesse who had less seniority than many other drivers. Suddenly, their plans appeared to be put on hold.

"I never saw that coming, Gloria. I was hoping I'd spend a lot of years driving those logging rigs for Timber Wolf. Now, I don't have a clue what I'll do. Clarksville isn't exactly a booming community. Even another trucker's job would mean we'd have to move to a bigger area," he said.

"We'll be okay. You'll see. If it means moving, I'm ready. I can get a waitressing job anywhere. I'll go where you go. We have enough money saved to give you time to look for another job."

Throughout the summer months, Jesse hunted for a job as far south as Concord, but it seemed that the trucking jobs were scarce, and he came up empty. In September 2008, he announced to Gloria that he had joined the military. The recruiter had offered a generous signing bonus, and the choice of several different areas he could focus his career in. Gloria thought that if it made Jesse happy, she would adjust to life as a wife of an enlisted man, but that wouldn't happen until his basic training was done with, several months later.

They were married in a small ceremony in Clarksville in front of a justice of the peace a week before he received his first assignment to Fort Benning, Georgia. He had decided to specialize in weaponry training because the pay grade was better than other areas, but then again, so was the danger involved.

In November 2008, he received news that he was being deployed to Afghanistan. The news was devastating to

Gloria, as she realized his assignment would likely be for a one or two year period. But true to her husband, she would remain at Fort Benning while he was away, keeping herself preoccupied with her new job in the mess hall at the base.

By March 2009, Jesse's leadership skills qualified him for elevation to sergeant, and he would be in charge of a five-man unit patrolling the streets of Bagram each day. Bagram, where thousands of allied troops were working and living in dust-filled tents, was the headquarters of the U.S. war effort in Afghanistan.

The world's most heavily mined country, Afghan landmines remained a deadly scourge for youngsters and troops alike. Jesse was aware of the thousands of mines that had already been removed, and the over fifteen thousand more still to go. Soldiers were warned not to stray from the beaten path.

He had never mentioned the landmine situation in letters to Gloria to avoid worrying her. It was estimated that it would likely take about one hundred years to clear all the mines in Afghanistan. As he patrolled the streets of Bagram with his unit, Jesse was well-informed about these silent killers, and he carefully protected his men from the mine zones, as they were called.

*   *   *

Sydney Fletcher's remaining teenage years, after the accidental hunting death of her father, were spent at La-Salle Academy, a Catholic school in Providence, Rhode Island. It was there that she met Bruce Malone, a baseball player on the varsity team, and an auto mechanic after school at his father's garage at Olneyville Square in the Olneyville section of Providence. For a guy who was six-foot-two inches tall and solidly built, Bruce was a gentle person, and sat next to Sydney in several classes in the business curriculum at LaSalle. The more she got to know him, the closer they were. He was very supportive of all her efforts to comfort her mother, who became virtually useless as she never accepted the loss of her husband years earlier. This depressive state brought on other ailments in her mother, and Sydney found herself having to care for her mother more every day. Any thought of college upon graduation was out of the question, as she needed to get a job to supplement her mother's income, which became unreliable at best. The string of ailments caused her to frequently miss days as a stock clerk at the East Side Market on Pitman Street. They lived in subsidized housing on Manton Avenue, and even with her full-time secretarial position at Adler, Pollack, and Sheehan, they barely eked out a decent living.

But Bruce was always there to perk her up when she became depressed at the constant care her mother required. He would take her to dinner at nice restaurants, buy her gifts at every occasion, and genuinely treated her with kindness. Sydney promised herself that one day she would lead a more luxurious lifestyle, something she imagined in the face of near poverty.

Bruce's inner struggles with repairing cars for the rest of his life were never discussed with Sydney. He believed she had enough problems of her own. But in late

2008, as he passed a storefront for a military recruiting office, he went in and signed up for the Marines. The recruiter had informed him that arrangements could be made for Bruce to get housing for a wife and a dependent parent. Incentives were ways in which recruiters would entice young men to consider joining the military, and the potential for college assistance along the way meant that Bruce saw an opportunity to develop a trade or a career beyond that of an auto mechanic in the family business.

In early 2009, he and Sydney were married at All Saints Memorial Church on Westminster Street in Providence. Bruce's family paid for the entire wedding reception at the Venus de Milo restaurant in Swansea, Massachusetts afterwards. The honeymoon would have to be delayed for a time because Bruce was scheduled for six weeks of basic training at Camp Lejeune in North Carolina first. He had been told that he would then be assigned to Fort Benning, Georgia pending his next assignment which had not yet been determined.

Meanwhile, Sydney and her mother were housed in an apartment at Fort Benning. Following his basic training, which Bruce found relatively easy, due to his athletic skills and excellent physical shape, he received word that he would be sent to Afghanistan for one year in late March. The news was crushing to Sydney, and she was lost at the thought of being isolated on a military base with the responsibility of caring for her ailing mother, and no means of socializing in an area of the country she knew little of. At least in Rhode Island, she had made friends at the law firm, and had become very accustomed to local venues. Bruce sat her down a few weeks before he was deployed.

"My military pay will automatically go into our checking account each month. The housing is free while I'm over there. I'll be gone no more than a year, maybe less if I'm lucky. Everything will be fine, I promise," he told her one night. She still had difficulty accepting his departure to a country in turmoil. She had an uneasy feeling when he left.

Bruce's plane landed in Kabul on March 23, 2009, and he was to report to the military camp in Bagram for further training and his assignment. That's where he met his unit leader, Sgt. Jesse Sokoloski. Jesse and Bruce hit it off from the moment Bruce was introduced to him. In the coming weeks, they patrolled the Bagram streets together on a daily basis, being ever so careful to avoid mines that were buried throughout the city.

Then, in the second week of April, Jesse's unit was assigned to a new war-torn section of Bagram where snipers had been shooting at and killing civilians. The Afghan military had asked for help from the U.S. forces to rid the area of these snipers.

Bruce was asked by Jesse to be the point person as the unit entered the area with its half-torn buildings and potholed streets. Bruce proceeded very cautiously, looking from side to side for any movement in one of the shattered buildings. Suddenly, he noticed a militant with a rifle dart across a building to his left. As he turned and headed for the building, he took his eyes off the road for a brief moment. That's when his foot stepped on a landmine and exploded.

Jesse, not far behind, ran to his aid. As he reached the limp body on the ground, a sniper's bullets hit him twice and he went down as well. Both of them were dead.

They had barely met, and yet, both died in the line of duty. Two lives that had so much to live for.

CHAPTER 28

DÉJÀ VU

Gloria had enthusiastically agreed to marry Richie, and they planned an October wedding. In late August, they found an adorable ranch house in Cape Elizabeth, just south of Portland, and rented the house with a one-year lease and the option to buy the house after a year at a fixed price less the rental payments already made.

A few days before they were set to move in, Gloria decided it was time to sort through the boxes she had piled in the hallway closet of her apartment. As she opened the first box, a solemn look appeared on her face. The box contained photographs of her and Jesse and his high school diploma. She started sorting the contents by placing each item on the kitchen table. Jesse had been good to her, especially when she carried a guilt complex about the death of Sydney's father at the hands of her own father.

She gently touched Jesse's military photo in full dress uniform, and tears built up in her eyes. She knew she had to finally let go, and clearly was ready for the next chapter in her life with Richie. She put the photo aside, and reached for the next item in the box, a newspaper clipping in the *Valley News* newspaper.

Two U.S. Soldiers Die In Kabul

April 11, 2009. Sgt. Jesse Sokoloski was killed on April 9th by sniper gunfire while attempting to reach a fallen comrade, Cpl. Bruce Malone, who had accidentally stepped on a landmine in the streets of Bagram, Afghanistan. Sokoloski, age 20, lived at Ft. Benning, Georgia with his wife, Gloria, before being deployed to Afghanistan in 2008. He graduated from Pittsburg High School in Pittsburg, New Hampshire in 2007. He was the son of Henry and Ruth Sokoloski, owners of the North Woods Trading Post in Pittsburg. Sgt. Sokoloski will be buried with military honors on April 16th, following a Mass of Christian Burial at 10 a.m. that day in the Farmham Memorial Methodist Church, Main Street, Pittsburg.

She vividly remembered the day of the funeral, a rainy day in Clarksville and Pittsburg. The thoughts that went through her mind that day were nothing short of despair. But suddenly, as if she had been hit by a lightning bolt, she grabbed the newspaper article and read it aloud to herself.

....*a fallen comrade, Cpl. Bruce Malone*

She jumped up from the kitchen chair and ran to her

bedroom. She looked on top of her dresser for the card Sydney had given her with her cell phone number on it. She then ran back to the kitchen, grabbed her cell phone and texted Sydney. Sydney was probably at work, so Gloria did not want to disturb her. A text message seemed more appropriate.

Quick question…what was your late husband's first name, and what was the date of his death in Afghanistan? I'll explain later. Gloria

Sydney had slept in on this day, and was also making plans with Drew to attend Gloria and Richie's wedding. When she turned her cell phone on as she prepared to have breakfast, she heard it buzz. She reached for the phone and read the text message from Gloria.

What a strange thing to ask, she thought. *Why is she asking me these questions, especially now?* Before she hit the reply symbol, she went into her bedroom closet and pulled down an old shoe box. In the box, she retrieved a newspaper article on Bruce Malone.

Landmine Accident Takes Life of Rhode Islander

Corporal Bruce Malone, a resident of Ft. Benning, Georgia, was killed on April 9th on the streets of Bagram, Afghanistan, when he accidentally stepped on a landmine. Cpl. Malone was part of an improvised explosive device team (IED) to unearth landmines placed in Bagram. Malone becomes the 190th casualty from IEDs. It is estimated that over 9000 IEDs are planted throughout Afghanistan. Malone is the son of Francis and Beverly Malone of Providence. He graduated from LaSalle Academy in 2006, and joined the

Marines in 2009. He had been in Afghanistan only a few weeks before the landmine incident. He leaves a wife, Sydney, and two sisters, Lucille Marciano of Smithfield, and Heather Cole of Greensboro, North Carolina. A military funeral will be held at 11 a.m. on April 25th at the Cathedral of St. Peter and Paul, 30 Fenner St., Providence. There are no calling hours.

She replaced the notice back in the box, and placed the box on the top shelf of the closet, and walked back to the kitchen. She hit the reply button and texted her reply.

April 9, 2009. His name was Bruce. What's going on? Syd

Gloria responded almost immediately.

I'll see you at the rehearsal on Friday. I have something to share with you, but it has to be face to face. Gloria

The wedding was set for two o'clock on Saturday. As tradition would have it, the wedding party would hold a rehearsal dinner following a walk-through at the church on Friday. Gloria refused to discuss her phone text with Sydney at the rehearsal itself, insisting she would do so that night at the restaurant. Sydney's curiosity almost got the best of her, but she reluctantly agreed.

At six o'clock, the wedding party gathered for dinner at the Rainbow Grill. Drew had agreed to be the best man, and Sydney the maid of honor. Local former high school friends made up the remaining bridesmaids and ushers. Rona Volpe was beaming as she sat next to Ralph and Diana Jones.

Gloria was nervous, and she had confided in Richie about the announcement she was about to make. He had tears in his eyes as he held her by the hand as she rose.

"I know this is very unusual, but as we toast our upcoming marriage tomorrow, I can't help but turn to my forever friend, Syd, someone I had lost, and finally found again, like it was meant to be. What we have been through, you and I, was not pleasant over the last ten years, but let me tell you, my dear friend, why this was meant to be."

She pulled a clipping from the side pocket of her slacks, and went on.

"Ten years ago, we both lost our husbands in Afghanistan, and life didn't seem to go too well for either of us. But, did you know that your Bruce and my Jesse were killed on the same day? And did you also know that my Jesse was shot by a sniper trying to get to your Bruce, who had hit a landmine? They were friends, Syd. Our husbands knew each other, and we never knew."

Gloria showed the clipping she had kept all these years to Sydney, and she stared at Gloria in disbelief.

"We may have been apart all this time, but we were closer together through them than you would ever imagine. They were friends, Syd, until they died. You are my closest friend, and you will always be my closest friend, until we die."

There wasn't a dry eye in the room as they hugged and cried in each other's arms. Richie and Drew were especially pleased to witness this touching display of friendship, and Richie had much to be thankful for as he shook Drew's hand with both of his.

* * *

If the next day's wedding was meant to be, could another wedding be far behind? Drew had made up his mind, and everything would come out this evening when they returned to the cabin following the dinner.

It was nine o'clock when they entered the cabin. Drew started the generator, and flipped on the lights in the living room. He walked to the fireplace which was all set up and ready to be lit, and got the fire going. Within minutes, the fire was blazing.

"I need the fire to be really good, because there are some things I need to burn in the fireplace tonight. Can you help me with that?" he asked as he faced Sydney.

"Sure, what are you burning?" she asked eagerly.

"Hopefully, we're burning a part of the past that needs to stay in the past. I need to know that there is no need any more for what I'm burning."

At that moment, he reached into a nearby closet and pulled out a brown trash bag. He carried it to the hearth in front of the fireplace and opened the bag. Sydney knew what was in the trash bag, as she approached him.

"I can explain," she said.

"I don't want an explanation. I don't need one. What I do need is a promise that these clothes are no longer needed, that what we have going here is far greater than what these clothes represent. I need to know that I will never see a blonde wig on that lovely black hair you have. I don't want to know who this person was. I just want to know the person I'm falling in love with who's standing before me right now."

Tears rolled down her cheeks for the second time

this night as she began to toss the clothes into the fire.

"You've known all along, haven't you?"

"No, not until the coincidences stacked up much too much pointing to you. I didn't think our relationship could ever work, until I heard about money the victims were starting to get in the mail."

"It might take a while, but I'll give it all back. I promised myself I would do this. I know what I did was wrong. And after I met you, and we started getting closer, I had to make things right again."

Drew reached for more clothes in the bag until it was empty.

"It was you who slipped that note under my door for me to leave Hunter's name on my windshield, wasn't it? That's when it really hit me that what I was doing was dangerous and foolish. You never gave up on me, did you?" she asked as she latched onto his arm.

"Some things are worth saving. I am in love with you, Sydney Malone, real estate agent, and I'm in love for only the second time in my life," he said.

"And I am in love with Drew Diamond, my savior and my soul, and I too am in love for only the second time in my life," she replied. "If I have stolen your heart, it will be the last thing I ever steal."

Could a second wedding indeed be in the forecast?

A Diamond for a string of pearls.

ACKNOWLEDGEMENTS

The little things that people take for granted often become key ingredients in my novels. But what I never take for granted is the support I continuously get from my family to produce a novel you simply choose not to put down until you're finished reading it. Leading the way in these efforts are my wife Pauline, and my three adult children, Barbara, David, and Julie. I could never write a successful story without their proofreading and copy editing, and certainly have welcomed their critiques every step of the way. And to Glenn Ruga, the founder of Social Documentary Network, and the Executive Editor of ZEKE Magazine, your formatting, newsletter creation, website maintenance, and keen eye in the design development of my covers, all have contributed again to my success in more ways than you could ever imagine. Your professional brochure, depicting all of my books, is above other brochures, and enables me to connect easily with my audience.

And to Jennifer Givner of Acapella Book Cover Design, you continue to create a book cover that attracts readers, exactly what a book cover should do. I am again indebted to you.

About The Author

Julien Ayotte was born in 1941, the fourth son of Gaston and Idalie (Donneau) Ayotte, in Woonsocket, Rhode Island. He graduated from Mt. St. Charles Academy in 1959. In 1963, he received a B.S. degree from the University of Rhode Island, followed by an M.B.A. in 1969, a Harvard Business School Management Development Program in 1978, and a PhD from Columbia Pacific University in 1992.

In his forty year career, Julien served as the Assistant Corporate Treasurer and Assistant Corporate Controller at Textron Inc. for eleven years, following nine years as a high school teacher in Bellingham, Massachusetts. He then served as a financial and investment consultant until becoming the executive director for a prominent Providence law firm, Partridge, Snow & Hahn in 1988-1989, followed by twelve years in a similar position for a much larger prestigious Worcester law firm, Mirick O'Connell, where he ended his career in 2002. During this fourteen year period, Ayotte also was an adjunct professor of finance and investments in the MBA programs at five universities in the Rhode Island and Massachusetts area.

He began to write his debut novel, *Flower of Heaven,* in 1987, but after completing ten chapters, he put it aside because of other commitments. He started writing again in 2001, and co-authored a financial planning book with Dr. Gerhard Harms, entitled *Wealth Building for Professionals. Flower of Heaven* was published in 2012, followed by the sequel, *Dangerous Bloodlines,* in 2014, *A Life Before* in

2016, *Disappearance* in 2017, and *Code Name Lily* in 2018. His sixth novel in seven years, *Diamond and Pearls,* was released in early 2020.

Julien is an avid golfer and tennis player, and a 2016 inductee into the Mt. St. Charles Athletic Hall of Fame. He also serves as a Trustee, Extra Ordinary Minister, Chair of the Parish Finance Council, and an altar server at St. Joseph's Church, Woonsocket, Rhode Island.

He resides with his wife of fifty-six years, Pauline, in Cumberland, Rhode Island. They are the parents of three grown children, Barbara, David, and Julie. He is still on track to write ten novels in ten years, and is more than half way toward achieving that goal.

Made in the USA
Middletown, DE
06 March 2020